Stranded on Mining Planet

A Predator Planet Universe Novella

Vicky L. Holt

Chapter 1

"Miner 56, status update," my aboveground handler buzzed in my ear. Three hundred meters of solid rock and metal crust, not to mention several thousand kilometers of space, interfered with our radio telemetry, but I could still hear him in spite of the static.

"Almost got it," I said, my voice straining from exertion. "The bearings feel sluggish. Are you sure Hastings completed maintenance last day cycle?" I used my grav-chisel to bang against the handwheel, which is *not* the recommended usage by the way, and tried again.

"According to the work log, yes, Miner 57 completed maintenance," my handler said. "Did you check if the latches were disengaged?"

Grumbling, I laid my grav-chisel against the shotcrete wall—I knew I'd need it again—and triple-checked the latches. "Latches disengaged. I'm getting resistance when I turn the wheel," I said with a grunt. I put my shoulders into it, but the wheel wouldn't move more than a few centimeters at a time. Sweat broke out on my hairline and under my arms. Glancing at my wrist, I felt my heartbeat speed up. "ETA for the last shuttle?" I hated that anxiety pitched my voice higher than normal. MP-13 was not the planetoid on which to show weakness.

"You've got plenty of time, 56," he said.

Assurances were great among friends where everyone trusted one another to tell the truth. But Marsel Granda wasn't my friend. The dynamics were complicated, especially after this last long rotation. And I noticed he didn't answer my question.

Head pounding from both physical and mental stress, I heaved again, pushing up through my feet and legs, my grav-mag boots anchored on the rock floor. The handwheel turned another four centimeters and slowed.

Muting my mic, I kicked against the huge metal door and screamed in frustration. One of my last duties before shuttling out was to seal the door to Tunnel CN 7. Normally, I'd spin the wheel until I heard the click of the inner latch and then type in the lockdown sequence. But something was wrong. Wishing I could swipe at the sweat on my forehead, I took a deep breath and blew it out on a sharp sigh.

"Hold the shuttle for me, will you?" I told Granda. "I'm going to grab the lube from Maintenance Supply and try to fix the handwheel."

"Copy that," Granda said, the static sounding worse. There must be another flare from MP-13's dying star, WD-237.

Trudging through the tunnels, my heavy steps reverberated as I walked. Running was preferred, but my boots weighed two kilograms. Each. I would get there when I got there.

Checking my wrist again, I swallowed as the countdown advanced. Granda better hold the shuttle for me.

I punched in the code for Maintenance Supply, waited for the green light and the chime, and pulled the door open. The auto-red flicked on bathing the closet with its red-orange glow. MP-13 was operating on minimum energy output since we were shutting down for the planetoid's winter.

I grabbed the can of lube and the long twizzler brush while I was at it and retraced my steps to Tunnel CN 7. Applying generous amounts of lube in the access points, I also shot into the latch bays and fished the twizzler brush inside, swishing it around. The ever-present mining dust played havoc with moving parts. Pulling it out, the lube dripped, darkening the thin layer of dust that covered the floor.

Tossing the can and brush aside, I pushed against the wheel again, and it picked up speed. With a final zip and click, the tunnel door sealed. I punched in the code and MP-13's automated PA system narrated the shutdown sequence.

"Tunnel CN 7 locked down," I said into my live mic, waiting for Granda's response. Static erupted in my ear and cut out. "Hold the shuttle. I'll be topside in seven minutes, thirty-six seconds," I said. A good little miner would put all the tools away first, but that bastard Hastings clearly hadn't done maintenance, and I needed to catch the last shuttle off Mining Planet 13. Being stranded on a planetoid while it entered its winter season was as good as a death sentence.

Hopefully, IGMC valued my work as one of the most experienced Retreat Mining engineers this side of the Pollack-Custer belt, not to mention the side project they commissioned me to do, and Granda's request to hold the shuttle would be granted.

Heart racing, I bent to switch out of my grav-mag boots and slide on my lightweight surface grippers.

"Granda, hold the shuttle! I'm coming!" I said between pants. I ran through the tunnels to the Personnel Lift, passing dark offshoots and abandoned machinery as well as piles of gear left behind by rushing miners. Yeah, we couldn't get off MP-13 fast enough.

Slamming the button for the PL, I cocked my head, waiting to hear Granda's grainy voice. "I'm in the PL," I said. "See you soon."

No static this time. No nothing.

Swallowing a lump, I stepped into the PL, pushed the close doors button, and rehearsed the route to the shuttle loading bay. With more time, I'd tidy up my private quarters and grab a vitamin loaf, but as it was, I congratulated myself for thinking ahead and packing my bag before my shift. I even had the presence of mind to leave it at the gangway.

The PL shuddered to a stop, and I pushed my way through the narrow channel before it slid all the way open. Running full tilt, I saw the pillows of dark gray burner plume that obscured the shuttle. Butter my butt and call me a biscuit; Granda had held the shuttle for me.

Scooping up my bag at the gangway without slowing, I raced up the ramp and broke through the cloud. Nothing looked more beautiful than the open shuttle door welcoming me inside.

I careened in, shoved my bag into the cargo tray, and strapped into my seat.

"Thanks, Granda," I said, huffing to catch my breath. "I 'preciate it."

Still no response, but I didn't care at this point. The shuttle door closed, the engines pulsed, and I closed my eyes and pressed into the back of the seat.

I always tried to prepare for the Gs, but I was never prepared.

Force pushed me so hard into my cushioned seat that its tufted fabric was visible in my peripheral vision.

Any second now, the shuttle would clear MP-13's strangled atmosphere, and I'd float against my straps. Any second now.

Alarms surrounded me in the fuselage. Designed to hold twelve people and their single IGMC-issued bags, it resembled any commercial transport with its industrial grade low-pile carpet in IGMC's colors, charcoal gray with crimson and navy accents, upholstered reclinable seats, molded light gray bulkhead and Galvanite-infused portholes. The "cockpit" in the bow of the shuttle was nothing more than a semi-enclosed space for the navigation system computer. I was its only occupant, and I was on the verge of total panic.

Lights on the navigation system blinked furiously as assorted alarms and beeps bounced around the cabin. The abyss of space out the portholes gave me no clues as to what was happening and judging by the absence of static in my ear for the past several minutes, Granda wasn't going to tell me, either.

"Granda, there's a problem," I said. "I think something ..."

A roll sent me flinging limbs outward, but the seat-straps held me in place. The shuttle's PA, calm as a bank teller, played a message on repeat.

"Stay calm. Shuttle preparing for emergency landing. Brace for impact."

Squeezing my eyes shut again, I tried to hug myself and tuck my legs in in spite of the hurdling shuttle and prayed the safety features worked.

Roaring whooshed around me, and then the startling ka-chunk, as if one had stepped on a pop can. After the crushing metal noise, there was silence.

Of the twelve seats in the shuttle, I'd chosen the one closest to the door, seat 4A.

A steady drip echoed inside the cabin as I stared at the seat in front of me, that technically shouldn't be. 2B. Vision shifting around me, I couldn't grasp the shuttle's new configuration, and I felt like taking a nap.

It had been a long-ass day, after all.

But a niggling thought hounded me every time I closed my eyes.

"Get out of the shuttle, Shay Leviticus," that thought said. Shaking off my foggy mind, I unbuckled my straps and stumbled to the side. The formerly neat seat arrangement was a twisted mess.

Emergency lights flicked in a racing stripe to the emergency hatch.

I paused before pressing the button; felt like I was forgetting something. Or many things. But that persistent thought nudged me forward, and I pressed the button.

Hissing noises jetted from either side of the hatch, and then it popped outward, hanging from its hinge.

Climbing out and over the hatchway, my grippers landed on planetoid soil, that strange mix of liquefacted regolith coating the coarse rocky underlayer.

My breaths sounded harsh in my ears, and I wanted to remove my helmet, but safety protocol training insisted I keep it on this close to the wreck. MP-13's oxygenated atmosphere could support human life, but it was thin. Breathing felt like a chore, and I was prone to headaches without support from my enclosed helmet and suit. I stumbled away from the crash, assessing for injuries with every step, but other than being shaken up, I was fine.

A good fifteen meters from the crash site, I turned to look at the smoking remains. I listened to my breathing change from exerted pants to slower, contemplative breaths.

Turning toward the mining base, I spotted the low-profile living quarters building, its taupe exterior the only visual relief from MP-13's ubiquitous charcoal color.

Sweaty hair plastered to my forehead, I decided to risk the headache while I hiked to the quarters. It was about sixty meters away. Helmet under my arm, I breathed in the chill air. MP-13 smelled like spent fireworks and looked exactly like what it was. A devoid rocky planet whose sky remained a starry night save for the haunting glow provided by the nearest gas giant. No plant life aboveground, no birds, no flying insects, no clouds, no sunshine.

Well, it wasn't accurate to say no clouds. The gas giant, PH-4RT, or Phart as we lovingly referred to it, temporarily shared its atmosphere in a Cthuhulian hug, the winds of Phart's rotation sending tendrils of breathable air to bathe MP-13 in a cocktail of oxygen, hydrogen, nitrogen, helium, and argon, supplementing its own fragile atmosphere. Planet and planetoid gridlocked in a summer fling of gravity and magnetism; it was a celestial physicist's dream. But my acting title was Retreat Mining Engineer, basically a glorified miner. To my understanding, unless something changed, the temporary arrangement would cause MP-13 to drag through Phart's atmosphere until the friction resulted in slowing MP-13's orbit while the gas giant's gravity drew it ever closer until it collided. Hence the haste with which IGMC had been mining precious iron ore from the planetoid, and also why IGMC hired me.

I swiped the trickle of sweat at the back of my neck and plodded through the regolith, my single goal the living quarters. Dizzy, thirsty, and confused, I suspected I had a concussion. That was the least of my worries, though.

Tidally locked MP-13 and Phart were riding their elliptical course farther from their star and headed into their winter season. Furious rotational winds would shed more oxygen and hydrogen onto MP-13's surface, but they would be frigid. If I was stranded on the mining planet, I was going to freeze to death in about six days.

Chapter 2

"Kezti battle cruiser docked," I spoke into my relay line. "No resistance witnessed outside the ship. Interior sonar scans picking up shots fired and vocalizations, but they're being quelled immediately."

"Understood, Drail," my superior, the Chak Dam Jai, said. "Maintain cloaking and return to the Dam's Vessel."

"Not yet," I said. "The Kezti's cruiser sent out a small vanguard. I want to see where they went."

"Very well," Chak Dam Jai said. "Signing off for now."

Skimming an invisible perimeter around the coupled ships, I focused my attention on the pair of vanguard-class fighters that disappeared around the curve of the gas planet, Hestra. Confident in their race's superiority over the poorly designed foreign ship, the Kezti fighters hadn't bothered to cloak theirs or cover their tracks with evasive maneuvers.

My people, the Dam Svai, patrolled this sector of the galaxy sporadically, and the presence of our long-standing enemies here begged the question why. The Kezti avoided us ever since we took control of the Causeway. The foreign ship wasn't impressive enough or exotic enough to warrant their interest, so something else must have lured them from their cloistered planet hideout.

The Kezti's battle cruiser and the strange, blocky ship were several spans behind me when I came upon a lone, dark satellite. At first, I thought it was debris from Hestra's broken moon, but closer inspection revealed its perfect lines and engineered planes.

Looking ahead, I could still see the radiation trail of the Kezti's vanguard. Risking time I may not have, I circled the satellite once, noting three simple docking bays that protruded from a bulging central mass prickled with dozens of what appeared to be communication arrays. I imagined it once glowed from signaling lights, but the gaping, jagged hole in the central sphere must have ended its usefulness.

"Chak Dam Jai," I haled my superior. "When were we in Hestra's sector last?"

"Six revolts past," he said. "Why?"

"Hoom. I'll explain when I return," I said. "Going dark."

Curiosity sent trills of excitement through the *pilo* sensors along my neck and shoulders. No wonder the Kezti were willing to risk getting caught by the Dam Svai. Something big was going on.

The strange ship was nothing special, just a huge metal box filled with an as yet undiscovered race, but the satellite looked like a halfway point.

Accelerating, I left the broken space station in my wake and pursued the faint trail of the vanguard fighters.

With Hestra's smoky glow at my right, I flew my recon ship only fast enough to remain at the same speed as the fighters.

We came upon Hestra's Handmaid at the same time, and I blew a low whistle.

The new race had been busy.

Hestra's Handmaid, once an empty, hazy planetoid, now boasted an energy signature worthy of a small civilization. What in Svai's Design had been going on here?

Before I could decide how close to get to the planetoid's surface, a flash of blue light erupted from one of the fighter ships. Sparks showered over the planetoid's surface, and then the vanguard ships zipped closer to their smoking target.

By now I was close enough to see the outline of several buildings, two launch pads, and the unmistakable signs of an immense mining operation with telltale scaffoldings, giant machinery, and the ugly scars of transportation cuts for roads. No thought for beauty in this place—only function.

A small smoking shuttle lay crumpled on the stony surface, and the vanguard fighters dipped and spun, leaving their parting shot as a calling card.

Caressing the thin atmosphere of Hestra's Handmaid, my ship cruised over the wreckage to leave the planet and follow the Kezti ships when I saw something.

The shuttle's hatch popped open, and two hands reached up to grasp the edge.

Holy Hestra of Svai's Design, I cursed.

Someone had survived the Kezti's assault.

Chapter 3

Thirty meters out from the wrecked shuttle I put my helmet back on. Maybe Granda had fixed the comms by now. "Granda, do you read?"

Nothing.

The ground shook beneath my grippers, and then I heard it. The shuttle's boom from its exploding unstable fuel cells knocked me to my knees and throbbed in my ear drums.

When I looked back, the shuttle was no more. Filaments of glowing material floated down in a surreal ashfall, and I scrambled back to my feet.

Conditions on MP-13 were getting worse and worse. I jogged the rest of the way, wanting the comfort and familiarity of my quarters to process what the hell had just happened to my day and how I was going to fix it.

Pressing my brow against the eye scan box, I waited for the beep and hiss of the dormitory's front door. When it slid open without a hitch, I exhaled a grateful breath.

The corridor's dim lighting indicated winter's reduced energy-use program had initiated in this building, as well, and I wondered if I'd have running water and a sustainable temperature. IGMC had to run some heating on MP-13's structures or they would need to be rebuilt every revolution.

In the "spring", the IGMC Initial Team arrived with flame throwers, propane torches, and pickaxes, and chipped thick layers of ice from the exterior surfaces. A week or so after the InitTeam landed, the spring thaw flooded the subterranean tunnels and filled the water reservoir deep in the mine. Once the tunnels were cleared, MP-13 was open for business, and the Room and Pillar Mining operation resumed.

My expertise was called upon during MP-13's autumn. Each new Room and Pillar site, once exhausted of its ores, transitioned to Retreat Mining. My demolitions team systematically took out the pillars, squeezing every last pebble of ore from the mine and closing out that particular tunnel system. Once completed, we sealed and locked the access doors and shuttled to IGMC's fleet ship, *Dynamo*, for some R&R until our next rotation.

We'd been mining MP-13 for three revolutions. IGMC estimated we had another five before conditions would be too dangerous and then the *Dynamo* would travel to the next destination.

But that was before today.

I'd sent my demolition team on the first shuttle of the day as a perk for their fine work yesterday. All I'd had to do was file some reports and seal and lock the tunnel.

Granda had been overseeing the rest of the employees' egress throughout the day while I'd been sending reports via the laggy RadWāv system. My reports kept kicking back, and Granda's temper had spiraled as he sat on his throne in the MidSat Station. The orbiting waystation was a comfy but glorified air traffic control tower from which Granda could call the shots on MP-13 and relay comms to the *Dynamo*. As waystation captain and fleet ship liaison, Granda held all the power and liked to flex his chops in numerous petty ways.

Today, he had taken perverse pleasure in telling me my reports were a full day-cycle late, but then reduced the base's bandwidth citing energy output restrictions. It forced me to bundle my reports in smaller digital packages and took me twice as long.

It was tempting to blame the shuttle's crash on his sociopathic tendencies, but as much of a jerk as he was, I hadn't thought him capable of attempted manslaughter.

The static-laden comms had been worse than usual. And then comms had disappeared altogether.

I opened the door to my quarters with my thumbprint and stepped inside, leaning against my closed door with a sigh. Home sweet home.

Kicking off my grippers, I padded across the charcoal gray carpet to my comms center. As the Retreat Mining engineer, I had access to better communications than most of the base occupants. Not that it had done me any good with Granda's stupid reindeer games.

Leaning over the holographic interface, I typed up the commands to connect with MidSat. Giant flashing letters spelled "Error: MidSat Not Found".

Frowning, I tried the much slower but more reliable StatWāv connection and pinged the Communications Officer on the *Dynamo*. Hopefully someone on the fleet ship could send a shuttle and pick me up.

It normally took a few minutes for StatWāv, so I turned on my teakettle and prepared a mug with a dollop of Krutenian honey and a tea bag. Wrapping my cold hands around my empty mug, I waited for the whistle of the kettle or the chime of the commlink, whichever came first.

Pouring hot water into my mug, I had time to stir the honey and steep the bag before the commlink announced a connection.

"Dynamo Communications Officer's Line, please leave a message."

Caressing the deep groove between my eyes, I puzzled over the recording. I had expected to at least talk with her assistant. Or an intern. Or the comms bot. Opening my mouth to speak, I didn't get the chance.

A half-nasal, half-buzzing voice plowed through the serenity of my quarters from my comms center speakers.

"This ship has been compromised," it said. "Who calls?"

Panic iced my veins, and I slammed my fist onto the Formica surface over which the holographic interface lay, equivalent to pressing the off button.

Tea sloshed over the rim of my mug in my shaking left hand, so I placed it on the counter with a trembling ceramic plinking sound.

Mind racing over possibilities, I retreated to the corner of my living room and pulled a throw over myself. Shivering from the inside out, I recognized I might be going into shock, and that could be deadly. Surviving a crash and then finding out the fleet ship had been "compromised" sent me into a tailspin. I put my head between my knees and breathed deep of the warm air inside my cozy blanket.

Inter Galactic Mining Corporation owned upwards of four thousand fleet ships. The fleet ships housed thousands of employees and docked hundreds of small explorer- and science-class ships. Spread across galaxies, IGMC also hired private security firms to escort the fleet ships in areas where mining operations competed with others for unclaimed resources. A behemoth of a corporation in a competitive industry, the idea that a fleet ship could have been compromised made no sense.

The deep voice had sounded garbled at first, and I realized translation software had kicked in.

Footage from the Ciliak Wars erupted in my brain.

No, no, the Ciliak had been wiped out. Shinterrans had joined forces with the humans and eradicated the giant bugs. Right?

But MP-13's orbit skirted the outside parameters of humans' presence in space. IGMC maximized its discoveries and wealth, and its reach knew no bounds. It was understood we would encounter more alien races. But I'd never once contemplated the almighty IGMC falling prey to any of them.

MidSat? Is that what happened to Marsel Granda? The waystation had no defenses; it was a high-tech condo with massive communications arrays.

The shuttle?

Had my shuttle been shot down?

Before I'd reached out to the *Dynamo*, I'd assumed sun flares had messed with the comms and maybe even the electronics on the shuttle, but I hadn't spelled it out yet. That's why I called the fleet ship; I needed more information.

But if aliens had taken over the fleet ship, then the waystation was a sitting duck, and the mining base was not far behind.

Taking over a mining planet that would be frozen into a solid ice chunk in a matter of days defied logic, but their reasons meant little to me. I was the sole human here, and thanks to my impetuous query, the invading aliens knew there was at least one not on the main ship.

Taking a deep breath, I looked at my little room with its tidy furniture and homey touches, like the mug stand and the metal puzzle cube, and no longer felt safe.

My loyalty to IGMC came at a high price, but they had a vested interest in my survival. Plus, I wanted to live, and the only way to do that was to fight with whatever weapons were at my disposal.

Which meant MP-13's entire armory. And my brain.

Yanking up my sleeve, I accessed the countdown feature on my wrist unit. I estimated I had, at most, two hours before they sent scouts after me. Setting it to a conservative sixty minutes, I pressed start.

Chapter 4

Guiding my ship to land behind a large outcropping of waste material dredged from the Handmaid's interior, I pondered my next steps.

As a general rule, the Dam Svai chose to remain aloof when two races collided. As stewards of the Causeway, we defended all travelers from pirates, but when disputes arose between similarly advanced races, we bowed out.

Whoever these new interlopers were, they had no knowledge of the Causeway, the Dam Svai, or the Kezti. Otherwise, their ship would have been logged with the Causeway Passage Authority. Judging by the massive presence of mining technology, they were no strangers to exploiting resources across space, however.

Technically, Hestra and her dying star Chamron, fell within the borders of the Dam Svai's governing stewardship. However, my people didn't patrol this far out often enough to restrict access. The Chak Dam Jai often said, "If they can get to it, let them have it."

Not known for initiative, the Kezti hadn't made any claims as long as I'd been in the Chak's service. It appeared they saw the interlopers' industry and wanted to capitalize on the enterprise. Had they not fired on a defenseless ship, I would wish them luck, though the planetoid was about to enter its frigid season, rendering all industry impossible. Perhaps the interlopers had discovered a way to work around the deadly temperatures, but I doubted it. My scans showed what I already discovered. There was but one life signature on the desolate planetoid.

"Chak Dam Jai," I said. "The Kezti vanguard-class ships fired on an unarmed shuttle. Sending the file now."

"Very well," he said. "Decloaking the Dam Vessel. We'll have the Kezti's captain arrested within a span."

"There is a survivor on Handmaid," I said. "I'm going to find them. When I do, they'll need to be shuttled back."

"I'm sure their captain will send one. Transmission confirmed," he said. "Happy hunting."

"Hoom. Indeed," I replied with a fanged scowl. Today's patrol was my last for the season. I'd hoped for a routine scan of these Outer Bounds and then to return to my vacation home in Svai-Tel. I was almost finished building my boat. The damned Kezti had a knack for ruining one's day.

Chapter 5

Tossing my throw, I sent a longing glance to my tea and ran to my tiny bedroom. My mind racing at a hundred miles an hour, I pulled out everything I thought I'd need in the next couple days for clothing, focusing heavily on socks. Tossing in an IGMC-issued jump shorts and sports bra set, as well as the custom NorClimb underlayers, I stuffed my tattered duffel. That's what I forgot on the shuttle: my IGMC-issued travel bag in which was my personalized communication tablet, favorite clothes, an honest-to-God paperback novel, and another of my metal puzzles. All reduced to molecules, now.

In the kitchenette, I jammed an excess of packaged meals (a throwback to my hungry childhood), a metal mug, my first-aid kit, and a clean towel into the duffel. For thirty seconds I stood in front of the water-filtration unit trying to figure out how much water I was willing to carry. I decided on three pouches; I knew every meter of this planetoid and its tunnels. Where I was going, I could access water.

With heart thundering in my chest, I took a last look at my homey space and grabbed my sidearm I kept near the door. Slapping the magazine in, I holstered it around my thigh and donned my bad-weather mining coat. Shoving my feet into my grippers, I snatched up my helmet and put it on, securing it at the neck of my Core Suit. Since the fiasco at the tunnel door, I hadn't had time to change into normal clothes. Turned out to be a good thing, after all.

Headed to the mines, I scanned the empty corridor both ways and paused at the door to the exterior, peeking out the window. MP-13 looked the same as it did thirty-five minutes ago: no sign of aliens or alien spaceships, but that meant nothing.

Jogging to the elevators, I pushed the subbasement button and adjusted the duffel bag over my shoulder while I waited.

The door opened with a ding, and I stepped in, pushing the 'close door' button with more force than necessary. Déjà vu.

"Computer, what's MP-13's status?" I said, accessing the base's artificial intelligence via my helmet mic.

"MP-13 is powering down all major systems in preparation for its winter season," the smooth female voice said. "Including HVAC-9 LS Unit Supply, all comm systems, S&R Bays 1 through 5, Power Bank Turbines 1 through 3, and wireless EG systems for all MEGA-Mechanics."

"What about the water supply and heating for the tunnels?" I asked.

"Water filtration and pumping stations at Low Energy Output levels, operating at five percent capacity. Subtunnel Heating set to three degrees Celsius. Current temperature in Access Hub is fourteen degrees and holding steady."

"Thanks," I said absently, mind already humming with plans.

"Pardon me, Miner 56," the Computer said. "But may I ask why you are still onplanet? System parameters indicate human life is not supported on Mining Planet Thirteen in the coming days and weeks."

I sighed.

"Yeah, that's a great question. I lost contact with Granda but made it to the shuttle in time. Then the shuttle malfunctioned under suspicious circumstances, and I crashed.

When I called the *Dynamo*, an alien answered and said the ship was compromised. So here I am."

"I would call that a significant bug in your day's program," the Computer said. "I am at your beck and call, Dr. Leviticus, should you need my assistance."

Taken aback by the AGI's offer, I paused a beat before replying.

"I appreciate that," I said, my voice cracking. Blinking fast, I looked up at the lift's ceiling and blew out a breath for good measure.

Whoever took over the *Dynamo* was focused on the fleet ship. Mining crews were notorious for their tough, scrappy attitudes and reluctance to submit to authorities, so I guessed there would be attempts at resisting the invasion on the ship. Depending on the ruthlessness of the alien race, such a resistance could last anywhere between an hour to two days. *God.* Was everyone okay? Was I the last human? Tightness in my throat and chest warned of a panic attack, but I couldn't panic right now. *Please let them be alright.*

Emergency hales would have been sent on IGMC's secret channel to the nearest known security outposts, but "rescue" could take weeks.

I guessed that the alien monitoring the comms station wouldn't have the authority to do anything about my incoming call other than report it.

If the aliens had reconnoitered, they would know MP-13 had been operating on a skeleton crew for the last seven day-cycles and judging by the timing of my last comms with Granda, the aliens may have planned their ship invasion to coincide with the arrival of the last populated shuttle. At that point, they would have taken out Granda's station. More and more I suspected my shuttle crash wasn't an electronic failure but rather the aliens' thorough eradication of the planetoid's populace.

Of course, my call signaled a missing link, and eventually the commanding force would want to make sure loose ends were tied up. That was me, Loose Ends.

But for now, I gambled that I had two days to secure the main subtunnels and ready myself to defend it. If worse came to worse, I'd have to go deep.

The elevator stopped with a jolt, and I pressed against the inner metal wall for steadiness. Doors sliding open at half-speed, I elbowed my way through and turned to the right down the huge rocky tunnel. The subbasement was twenty meters below the Access Hub and housed the lesser-known supply areas of the mining base. Notably, the armory.

IGMC protected their interests, sometimes in unexpected ways, but the bottom line was investment. They invested money and technology in the things they projected would bring the most income.

MP-13 was an experiment. With the standard presence of typical ores in predictable amounts and the operating costs of mining this far from the Pollack-Custer belt and for only three-fourths of a revolution, IGMC barely made a profit. On ore.

Jogging through the tunnel, my coat flapped behind me, and my duffel thumped against my back. My footsteps echoed in the huge chamber; it was never this quiet down here. With ventilation systems and heavy equipment deactivated, now the vast area created a steel drum effect; every drip, every footfall, every panted breath was weaponized into a reverberating gunshot of sound. And in between the sound bursts, the stillness of death. I reached the armory and scanned my thumb.

Huge metal door sliding on its track, the room's light switched on, and I stepped inside. The explosives vault drew my gaze first.

As lead Retreat Mining Engineer, I had access to everything required to blow shit up, especially rocks. Mentally mapping the weak spots on the mining base, I selected several Short Burst options from among the packages, as well as a few medium range charges and of course, two of the Boson Gelignite stacks, colloquially known as Big Guys. These I put in a separate case pulled from the shelf; it was lined with a protectant, though quite unnecessary, since the detonating materials were stored in a separate one. Counting off to myself, I filled both cases and closed them with satisfying clicks.

Next, the handheld weapons grid.

For a moment, I thought about Jainson. He was the Armory Custodian and usually the person I'd account to for the items I was taking. If anyone would defend against an alien assault, Jainson would. Guess I'd have to figure that out later, assuming the 'compromised' ship wasn't blown to smithereens. Throat suddenly dry, I swallowed. *Dammit.* All my colleagues on the ship. Head bowed, I paused to let anguish flow into me, and then back out on a slow exhale. *Focus.*

Hiding in the tunnels, I wouldn't need more firepower than short range weapons, but since I had room in my duffel, I went ahead and grabbed a dismantled Entropy Gun. I stuffed as many boxes of ammo as I had room for after the two smaller caliber guns I'd stowed.

Leaving the armory, I entered the lockdown code and humped it farther down the corridor toward the Spoke Tunnel, my duffel and two cases weighing me down with an extra twenty-five kilograms. Checking my wrist unit, I saw I had forty minutes left. With a silent curse, I dropped my bag, then opened the cases side by side.

Using some mental gymnastics, I stilled my trembling hands, pretending it was testing day back in ordnance school. My goal was to obscure the tunnels where I would be hiding out from prying alien eyes, but if that didn't work, my strategic blasting should funnel them the direction I wanted them to go: in a circle and far away from where I would be. The caveat emptor being that I didn't trap myself underground as a result.

Placing two medium range explosive packets at either side of the corridor, I stuck the detonating fuse-picks into the center. I synced their miniaturized servos with my detonator and grabbed the cases, running to the next spot.

Craning my neck to scope out the tunnel joists, I chose a smaller tunnel. The last in a series of three, if I caved it in, searchers wouldn't immediately recognize it because of its adjacence to a room my team and I cleared a couple weeks ago. Seeing a huge wall of rubble, they would choose between the two open tunnels which curved all the way around and emptied into the hall where the bank of elevators landed. It would buy me hours, if not a couple days. Because rubble from the smaller detonation would obscure the emergency egress panel.

A human-size chute, the passageway's entrance was protected from blasts by an engineered blast vent reminiscent of an oven hood. Its flared sides directed rocky debris away from the opening but was strong enough to hold tons of rock if it flowed over the top.

Satisfied my Short Bursts were well-placed, I returned to the Spoke Tunnel, grabbed my stuff, and ran full bore down the tunnel. Reaching the end, I punched in the code to shut its entrance and then dropped my bag and the cases, resting my hands on my knees.

Panting, I looked at my wrist unit. Eight minutes left.

Having caught my breath, I stood upright and looked at The Hub.

IGMC had mining down to a science. Employing the highest caliber engineers and newest technological innovations, they were canvassing the reaches of space to mine the elements.

MP-13's blueprints were similar to hundreds of others with one teensy difference.

A first wave of mechanical engineers, civil engineers, city planners and explosives technicians would scope a planet or planetoid, draw up plans and execute the same layout at every location.

Surface quarters for admin buildings and dormitory complexes, the shipping and receiving platforms, the storage facilities, launch pads, and strip-mining grid were built first, and then the Engineer Hub was built second.

Installed hundreds of feet underground, The Hub consisted of elaborate computers and monitors, communications, an R&D lab, a self-sustaining cafeteria and several small private rooms with hygiene facilities. From The Hub, eight spokes radiated outward but to varying levels.

My strategic blasts would keep scouts far away from The Hub unless they were neurotically curious. The only way in was Spoke Tunnel, and nothing could come through that door or the two-point-four-meter-thick walls.

Taking stock of the silent Hub, I pondered my next steps. Worst-case scenario, they find me down here and try to break through Spoke Tunnel. If they managed that, they'd have to send troops down every spoke of the wheel and into every room to catch me. *Dammit.*

There wasn't really a choice.

I had to go deeper. I had to take the dark tunnel to the MP-13's engine room. There were only three people who knew about it: Marsel Granda, the *Dynamo's* Captain Mear, and me, Shay Leviticus.

That's right. Planetoid MP-13, IGMC's latest experiment, had an engine. IGMC called it a Sphere Ship, and if it worked, I'd be set for life.

Whatever alien race had compromised the fleet ship had no idea what they'd stumbled upon, and it was up to me to make sure they never found out.

Grabbing my gear one last time, I checked my unit to see there were five minutes left, and I headed to the dark tunnel. Unmarked, unlit, and inaccessible to everyone except me and a couple others, the dark tunnel ran parallel to the number Five spoke. Five ended at a door marked 'Storage Auxiliary' and if anyone managed to access the triple lock, they'd find caskets of expensive and exotic materials. Suitable as a decoy for most people or aliens, I hoped.

Eye-scan complete, the dark tunnel door slid up, and I stepped over the threshold with my stuff. Jogging down the sloping tunnel, I used my helmet bulb to light the way, though it was empty of obstacles. It served as the only entrance to MP-13's engine room.

My wrist unit beeped, and I knew the hour was up. Once I reached my destination, I could patch into the Hub's communications and security camera feeds and see what I was up against, but I wasn't worried yet.

Thirsty and tired though, yes.

At the end of the dark tunnel stood another door, a simple metal one with no markings, and in front of it, a black mat. Standing on the mat, it recognized my weight distribution in my shoes, and the door lit up with screens. One designated where to rest my forehead, the other where to place my hand, palm to the door.

Identifying features analyzed and cleared, the door swung inward without a sound.

It'd been several weeks since I'd visited the engine room, as Retreat Mining had taken up most of my day-cycles, but everything looked and sounded normal, as I expected.

IGMC wasn't slated to start the Sphere Ship until after the winter season, but I was ahead of schedule. The other engineers and explosives techs weren't aware of my second field of expertise. Honestly, no one was, because it was new. In addition to my responsibilities as Lead Retreat Mining Engineer, I was also IGMC's sole Planet Propulsion engineer, and if I got MP-13 to break orbit and strike out on its own, IGMC had promised to remunerate me enough credits to set me up for life, as well as that of any future children, grandchildren and great-grandchildren.

Growing up in a scrappy neighborhood with a hungry belly made the promise seem like something out of a fairy tale, but God knew I'd worked hard to get here.

At my entrance, the room's lights grew in brightness until every monitor, console, computer housing and cable were revealed. Stowing my gear in a wheeled cart for the purpose, I shed my coat and draped it over the chair.

Leaning over the console, I entered the commands that would patch me into all the cams across the mining base. The huge monitor to my right showed a grid of dozens of camera feeds from every sector, and I scrolled along them with my finger until I reached the surface cams.

Expanding the view, I zoomed in as close as I could to the empty plain where the shuttle had crashed, but the cameras weren't trained in that direction. I could see a black smudge where some debris had fallen, but otherwise was blind to the crash site. Flipping through other surface cams, I saw the empty launch pads, the inactive S&R Bays, and the forlorn low-slung dormitory building. All was still, and in other circumstances, I could imagine the humor of a tumbleweed blowing across the dusty planetscape.

Scrolling the screens, I found the shuttle dock feed and stared in alarm. Two ships.

Accessing the playback feature, I rewound.

I saw the two ships, pointy and threatening, land as bold as you please on one of the shuttle docks.

Staring intently, I watched four hulking aliens as they disembarked, two from each ship, walking upright on two legs, holding what I assumed to be weapons in one set of arms while letting the other set swing casually by their sides. Armor or chitin covered their bodies, and their blocky triangle-shaped heads, or helmets, sat on wide shoulders without benefit of necks. Nodules arose from their heads and along their shoulders and top set of arms.

A cave rat darted from beneath the ramp and ran across their path, and one of them opened fire, the rat disappearing in a cloud of dust and smoke. I grimaced. Being as the feeds were black and white, that wasn't dust. Black scorch marks stained the ramp.

Dread, sick and fat, rolled in my gut, and I looked away for a second, feeling tears pool in my eyes.

When they paused at a control station and obliterated its contents, the console and lonely chair where Emmet or Chryslo usually sat and joked with the waiting passengers, they confirmed my suspicions. Debris and shrapnel exploded, and the metal hut dented with more shots. Once again, I thanked God the rest of us were already on the ship—but who knew? Maybe they had it worse than I did. What if ... what if the rest of these giant insectoids had obliterated everyone onboard?

I clutched at my chest, feeling dismay and fear war with each other until I could compose myself. Checking the time stamp, I realized they'd landed right about the time I was in the armory stashing cases with explosives. That meant they were a lot closer now. *Objects in mirror are closer than they appear.*

"Hey, uh, Computer?"

"Yes, Dr. Leviticus?"

"Remember that bug you mentioned?"

"Of course. It was my attempt to empathize with your current situation."

"Well, the bugs just got literal," I said. "Don't mind the subsequent detonations."

"Impending detonations noted," the Computer said.

I didn't need another excuse. I armed my detonator and pushed the command button that would fire every charge simultaneously.

"Let the flames begin," I said into the cold room. The computer didn't respond.

The slightest tremble rippled up through the floor and then stilled.

Entering a macro-program, I set the computer to alert me when motion-sensors were triggered anywhere on the mining base. Devoid of animal life bigger than the cave rats, the alarms would notify me when the aliens breached the tunnels.

For good measure, I opened up every camera feed and dialed back a few minutes. I needed to see where every single one was on this godforsaken rock.

Tabbing feed after feed, I quickly surfed blank screens. Nothing, nothing, nothing, there!

Heart in my throat, I saw a different race of alien in shiny armor and a domed-off helmet jogging the hall in the dormitory. Checking the time stamp, it was only minutes after I'd entered the elevator and taken it to the sublevel.

I watched in fascination as he stopped before *my* door, jiggled the knob, then pushed his way in. Why my door out of all the others? Oh, hell no he didn't.

Making a fist, I leaned forward.

He walked in and stopped as if running into an invisible wall. He disappeared farther into my apartment. Without feeds in the apartments, I wouldn't see what he did next, but a stirring of anger fluttered in my belly at the violation.

Movement in my peripheral caught my eye; a different screen showed a bug stalking the dorm hallway. He was following the guy with the domed helmet. Now I was just plain curious. What would happen next?

Tension flexed my shoulders as I watched the bug stride on its thin legs and its head turn side to side, as if unable to see straight ahead. With its giant bulbous eyes, I could only guess at its capabilities. It slowed when it reached my place, the door having swung back but not quite closing.

It pushed the door open with its long weapon, and I half-expected the other alien to tackle it to the ground. But no, it ducked into my place, and I lost sight of them both.

Dialing the video forward at slow speed, I waited until my door opened and found myself exhaling with relief when the alien more resembling a human peered out into the hall, leading with his newly acquired long gun.

Riveted by the mini-drama, I shook myself from staring at the humanoid armored-up alien and resumed surfing the feeds. There were so many cameras, and only a handful of aliens to account for, that I lost track.

The Victor, I decided to call him, was moving fast. Whereas the bugs, every time I caught sight of their strange stumping walk, looked more methodical.

Frowning, I pulled up the surface feeds once more and scanned the last hour's worth of footage as quickly as possible, searching for a different ship.

Nothing.

As long as IGMC had been here, we'd never seen nor heard of aliens in this sector and certainly not on MP-13. I doubted the Victor lived here. More like he landed his ship away from any of the cameras and entered the base on foot.

Scouring footage again, I cussed. Staring at the grainy feeds made my eyes cross. But then it occurred to me to trace my own path from the crashed shuttle, or what I could see of it.

I pulled it up and watched, a strange otherworldliness settling over me as I watched myself, bedraggled and maybe even a little disoriented, stumbling across the regolith. Rather than watch myself all the way to my dorm, I kept my attention on the video waiting for something.

Sure enough, the Victor finally appeared on screen, and it didn't take a rocket scientist to see that he was following me. Now that I had a lock on him, I could run the tracking bot to find where he appeared.

Just as the bugs engaged in a methodical search, he moved in measured, careful steps.

But after he emerged from my apartment, he raced.

The bot lost him.

I didn't know what to think. Why did his slow search morph into a race down the corridor, out the building, and into the "streets" behind the dormitory?

Unable to focus, I stood up and rubbed my lumbar and scowled at the lonely engine room. By now I should have been halfway to the *Dynamo* and flipping off Granda in his high tower. I sighed and looked at my grippers. We weren't friends, but if he'd been attacked and killed, it was a shame. Tightness in my throat signaled a bout of crying was right around the corner, but I couldn't afford grief just yet.

I wiped my eyes and my forehead and then walked to the switch plate on the wall, dimmed the lights, and punched in my code to open the gigantic metal sliding panel that obscured the planet's propulsion device.

If someone were to bring up such technology in casual conversation, aside from sounding like a lunatic, their listeners would probably expect a massive glowing orb of nuclear radiation energy powerful enough to blind onlookers and cause massive exposure to cancer-causing toxic waste.

But they'd be wrong.

When IGMC contacted me about my post-doc paper on planet propulsion physics, they'd led with a generous "introduction fee", a no-strings-attached stipend, if I would entertain the pleasure of their audience for a couple days and go over my equations with their lead physicists and a handful of their corporate executives.

At the time, I had loans to pay off and insane debt from, ironically, IGMC's engineering college. Of course, they knew that when they offered. It wasn't a leap to go from finally feeling recognition for my work to being courted with a significant offer I couldn't refuse.

Staring into the blue-cast room on the other side of the Galvanite-infused radiation-proof glass, I marveled at the beautiful pulsing field contained within a suspended Galvanite tesseract. The tesseract was constructed of hollow Galvanite-metal tubes, as if a kid had been playing with PVC pipes and connectors, but the tubes were filled with Outer Gas.

Discovered around the time I was a sophomore in engineering college, Outer Gas was an element found in the outer reaches of the galaxy by two separate corporations.

IGMC and its rival, Space Core Technologies. Naming the gas was still in dispute, but the bottom line was Outer Gas was the first real proof that the Mirror Universe might be a thing. Outer Gas behaved in many ways like Nitrogen, but for lack of a better definition, was kind of like the opposite of Nitrogen.

At any rate, it was non-reactive with Galvanite, and better yet, it shared an interesting relationship with dark miasma.

My hands on the cool glass, I let my focus go soft as the enormous viewing window before me flowed with its blue light, as if the large cell room was an aquarium.

Beeping sounded from the workstation, and I snapped out of my reverie.

"Movement Detected," the smooth female voice sounded in the engine room.

"We've got company, huh?" I said.

"If by company you mean invited guests in preparation for a lighthearted social gathering," she said. "Then no."

I shook my head with a humorless laugh. I was still getting used to the artificial general intelligence that IGMC insisted I use down here. "No, this isn't a social call," I said. "You got that right."

I found the camera feed and frowned. They'd picked up motion, all right, but it was from a defunct tunnel a full two kilometers from the main mining operation. I didn't even know we had cameras out there.

Adjusting the light sensitivity, I saw two figures grappling with each other. One was the praying mantis-like alien, but the other the Victor. He was huge with shoulders nearly spanning the width of the old tunnel and arms twice the width of the bug aliens' spindly legs.

Pulling up map files, I tried to find the oldest ones from before, when IGMC first scouted the planetoid and plotted out where to blast, dig, and pour.

Keeping an eye on the fighting aliens, I scoured a map from four revolutions ago. I zoomed in and found the sector the camera was in.

"Do you have a name, Computer?" I asked.

"You may call me DAPHNE," she said. "It stands for Demolition and Propulsion Hyperconnected Network Entity."

"DAPHNE, indeed," I said with a smirk, leaning closer to find the sector. "This could be the beginning of a beautiful relationship."

Chapter 6

Exiting my ship, I powered it down and secured the hatch, climbing up the outcropping of rocky talus, gaze fixed on the crumpled vehicle smoking on the plain below. I'd seen the hands at an opening, but where was the survivor now? Using binoculars, I searched the area surrounding the crash and zoomed in on footprints leaving the crash site. I stowed my binoculars and found a sloping pathway down the outcropping.

I was not yet five steps down when a percussive blast rocked up from my boots, and I swayed a moment. Alarmed for the survivor, I scrambled over the nearest pile and looked on as ash particles floated gently to the ground. The vehicle was gone in a latent explosion.

Extracting my binoculars again, I scanned the dusty plain for the footprints. Finding them, I tracked outward until I saw the black figure looking back at the site. From this distance, they looked small and dejected, posture indicating defeat. But then they turned on their heel and marched forward again, aiming for the long, squat building with a flat roof.

I released a relieved breath. The survivor yet lived. Not wishing to alarm them, I decided to fall back and wait until they had composed themselves from what was, no doubt, a frightening experience.

Glancing around the desolate area, I could appreciate the interlopers' industry on their large settlement on the far side of the plain. Their buildings looked well-constructed, if ugly.

They were plentiful as well. Staying well behind the survivor, I noted the variety of buildings and guessed at their purpose.

The launch pads were obvious; the Dam Svai had similar. Buildings standing near huge machinery must be related to the mining operation in some way, perhaps storing the ore or machines to refine it. The long and squat building boasted a line of rectangular windows along its entire face, suggesting a living quarters for several hundred persons. Taller buildings to the west of the living quarters sported dome roofs and many skinny poles, suggesting receivers or transmitters, or both, for communication.

Nearing one such building, I detoured to inspect it more closely, noting the survivor had entered the doorway of the flat building. Satisfied they were not seriously injured; I indulged my curiosity to discover the purpose of this cylindrical tower. I pressed on the door, and it pushed open without resistance. Odd, considering the survivor had performed a ritual to open the door of their building. I ducked inside, seeing that the circular room contained a series of tall cabinets, one of which was open, revealing a coat and boots. To the side began a flight of metal steps, and I placed one boot on the bottom step, testing its strength to bear my weight. In the absence of creaking or straining noises, I decided to trust the stairs with my weight, though clearly, they were built for persons smaller than my race.

The staircase wrapped along the inside wall and ended in an entryway in the ceiling. Looking up, I followed the flight and reached the second floor. This room had banks of computing systems and windows that ringed the entire circumference. The glass must possess a cloaking feature because the windows were not obvious from the outside.

My steps echoed on the bare floor as I walked along, curious about the strange markings on the computing machines, but impressed with the view of the mining base. "Hoom." From this vantage point, it appeared the construction and placement of this building was intentional, as the entire settlement was within view. Even the farthest part of the base, the strip mine, was observable.

I imagined this building must normally house a commanding officer or Dam Jai, an acting head for the settlement. If not concerned about creating beauty, this race at least appeared organized and orderly. Bemused, I shook my head and smiled, reaching out to knock against the metallic casing of the nearest computing machine.

Crackling and buzzing emitted, and I flinched back. I heard a voice, female, say words, and then another voice that sounded lifelike but studied. A recording? Cocking my head, I tried to make out the words when a Kezti's grating voice overrode the message.

"This ship has been compromised," he said. "Who calls?"

Chamron falls! The survivor must have pinged their ship. The Dam Svai Legion would restore their ship's command, but the Kezti were ruthlessly sore losers.

The noise evaporated as if it were never there, and the empty building sounded even more silent. Knowing someone from the ship had escaped their control, if only for a few spans, would grate on the Kezti's High Commander like a rock in a boot.

I leaped to the opening of the stairwell and jumped several steps at a time. Kezti High Command would send the vanguard ships back to finish their dirty work. Swallowing another curse, I realized the survivor's time was up.

Racing out the door, I loped toward the low building, scanning the sky for sign of the vanguard ships. None yet. At the entrance to the low building, I saw an eye scanner. That's how they opened the door. When the vanguard ships arrived, would they bomb the entire base, or land and hunt the survivor?

What I knew of the Kezti, they always preferred the path free of rocks. But vanguard ships weren't outfitted with enough gravity bombs to obliterate a mining base of this size.

Grim reality settled over my shoulders. They would land their ships and hunt.

But they did not yet know that I was here with a mission of my own.

Studying the layout of the base, they would probably land near the launch pads and systematically search the area location by location. Working their way orbitwise, they would find the building where the survivor entered it.

Waiting to see when they arrived, I hid myself behind a nearby stand of metal boxes and watched. The surviving person was safe until the Kezti landed.

The whine of engines caught my attention, and I spun to see the Kezti ships approaching from over the mountains.

They landed on the shuttle docks. *The path free of rocks.* The docks were far enough away that unless they used binoculars, they wouldn't see me yet. Two hunters emerged from each of the two ships.

Chamron falls. If I blasted my way through the door to bypass the scanner, the Kezti would know someone else was here. I preferred to remain an unknown quantity. Trusting the survivor had the sense to hide and hide well, I sprinted the length of the building to its corner and rounded the end, keeping my steps light and staying out of their line of sight.

I would still have to make my own entrance, but it would be in a less visible place.

The building's windows faced the shuttle dock, but once I rounded the end, the walls were solid. I ran to the next corner and turned and saw that the rear of the building had no windows or doors, but a series of metal boxes a click apart. Probably some sort of ventilation or power system.

Investigating farther, I discovered a stairwell leading into the lower level of the building. This demanded an eye scan as well, but I was out of time. I blasted the scanner with a single jolt of my helix weapon; it sizzled the electronics, and I was able to pry the door open with my claws and brute strength.

Ducking under this door as well, I was pleased to stand upright inside, my helmet mere strets from brushing against the ceiling. Down here, a narrow dim hall stretched as far as the eye could see with panels placed in tandem with the large boxes outside the building.

Searching the wall behind me, I spied an interior door lacking locking mechanisms, and sighed in relief.

Pulling the door open, I listened but heard nothing yet. I poked my head through and found a corresponding stairwell to the one outside. Taking the steps at a run, I reached the main level and peeked through the window placed inside the door. A beige empty hallway lay on the other side.

With careful movements, I opened this door, again checking for noises or smells. Still nothing.

A smooth floor covered in soft material like rambul fur quieted my boot steps. Its dark color mimicked the black rock outside, and I suppressed an inner sigh at the dismal environment. Was there no relief from the desolate views of Hestra's Handmaid?

Concerned the Kezti would head directly to the low building, I picked up my pace and ran through the short hallway headed for the front of the building where the windows were.

At the corner, I stayed out of view but looked through the glass in the direction of the launching area. After a moment I spied the hunters emerge from the first of the two giant warehouses. Good. They were searching in a grid, and for the time being, staying together in a single unit.

Flaring my nostrils, I tried to detect the odor of the survivor and caught a faint whiff of burnt materials. There it was. I walked, hunting the smell down, finding it strong in front of one of the plain tan doors on the right-hand side of the long corridor.

Testing the knob, it resisted, but I forced it, and the door opened at my nudge. Stepping inside, a fragrance of citrus and sweet syrup hit my nose with the force of a weapon. Shocked, I stood still and let the aroma surround me, sneaking its fragrance through the air vents in the side of my helmet.

I'd been on Causeway Patrol for two revolts now and had forgotten the refreshing scent of lama fruits in the spring. I'd planted lama trees at my vacation home.

Shaking myself, I growled. Had an enemy waited within, I'd be a dead Dam Svai now, not having entered with more caution. But the room was empty of life.

At my left was a standing light unit, off, but directing its face down at the furniture one surmised was for sitting. Across the furniture lay a wondrous blanket, woven throughout with every color of the light spectrum out of a soft and pliable fabric reminiscent of the domesticated peths the Dam Svai bred for rambul wool. Lifting it to my air vents, I smelled the survivor and deemed her a woman. The loops of wool retained her warmth; she'd left not strokes before my arrival.

I should leave now, but first I must find the source of the lama fruit scent. It would take but a moment to satisfy my ever-present curiosity. A low table in front of me held a lone, dying plant. A bank of electronic boxes must be the woman's communication and information-gathering center, and a counter separated the sitting area from the cooking area. On the counter sat a cylinder filled with warm liquid. Drawing closer I knew I'd discovered the aroma's source. Breathing deep, I relished it.

Turning to go, my gaze snagged on a shiny, metallic device with interlocking pieces. I pocketed it on a whim and strode to another doorway, finding the sleeping quarters of this small space. The fabric on the bed was wadded into piles and clothing lay strewn about. She had left in a hurry, judging by the warm beverage sitting untouched behind me on the counter and the opened drawers with items spilling out. But where would she go?

The Kezti had destroyed her only way off-planet. Every building would be searched top to bottom and back again until she was found.

She must know of a hiding place.

It had been many a long revolt, but I had visited Hestra's Handmaid before. Judging by the layout of the buildings and the location of the strip mine, waste rubble, and ore elevators, these beings had utilized the existing tunnel network to access ore deposits and built their base around them.

If memory served, there was an elaborate cave system fifty clicks from the general area where this building was constructed. I could access the tunnels from there without alerting the Kezti to my presence, find the woman by tracking her scent, and escort her back to her ship once the Chak Dam Jai informed her captain to send another transport.

The snick of a gun clicked behind me, and I realized I'd lingered too long in the woman's dwelling.

"Traz-Ger shines on me today," the gravelly voice said, invoking his wrathful god. Kezti hunters endured elaborate ritual surgeries to enhance their bodies for war, one of them being the severing of their larynx band. As a result, their voices sounded like shaking a metal tumbler full of orpentine rocks.

Hands raised, I turned to face them, finding only one.

He saw my searching gaze and spoke.

"My brothers suggested we split up," he said. "A wise decision allowing me to intercept you."

Thoughts racing, I decided to lie first.

"Hoom. You found me," I said. "Are you going to kill me or take me as a prisoner of war?"

His laugh hurt my ears, rough and disjointed as it was.

"There is no war," he said. "Only the meddling oversight of the Causeway by your people." His gray and green-striped head bobbed as he spoke, the antennae bouncing as he narrowed his two bulging spherical eyes at me. "I will wait for my brothers to decide what to do with you."

Stilling my breaths, I kept a steady gaze on the Kezti, hoping they would now leave the woman, assuming it was I who had garnered their attention from the comm.

"Do you think the lazy Kezti are stupid?" he asked while tilting his wedge-shaped head. "I see your pulse slow from the disgusting blood-tunnel in your neck. I sense the chemicals released by your concern for the female whose essence floods her living space. We know she is yet here, and we will find and take her in recompense for the spoils your Chak Dam Jai denied us with his interference."

Falls. Their keen senses picked up every nuance of emotion, but I kept my expression neutral anyway. Sneaking around Hestra's Handmaid had been my first choice. But to defend another race who had no history or quarrel with either the Dam Svai or the Kezti was my greatest joy and pleasure.

A sudden rumble thrummed up through the floor, catching both of us off guard. Perfect.

Dropping without warning, I kicked out my feet and swept the Kezti's leg stalks out from under him and slammed my armored elbow across his unstable weapon. It fired into the wall then spilled out of his grasp as he scrambled to regain balance.

Snagging it before it hit the ground, I used his own weapon to smash him between the eyes as I leaped to my feet, bashing him again in the thorax for good measure. My assault hadn't killed him, but as I watched green goo ooze from the split in his abdomen, I knew he would remain unconscious long enough for me to find the woman before his brothers did.

Panting, I stepped over the Kezti, bringing his weapon with me. Kezti long-range rifles were prized for their accuracy and fine machining but were not effective close-range combat tools. Thank Hestra.

Checking the corridor, I spared no glance for the cozy room behind me. What I sought was elsewhere, and I needed to find her ... fast.

Shutting the dwelling's door behind me, I retraced my steps through the hallway to the rear of the building, took the stairs to the lower level, reentered the door to the service hall and exited the door for which I'd blasted the electronics.

Most of Hestra's Handmaid's surface characteristics had been obliterated from construction, but the distant mountain range remained the same. Using it as a guide, I hiked over a hill of rubble, past more ugly buildings and onto a rocky plain. Checking behind me often, I had seen no sign of my enemy's companions, but had crouched in open areas and chosen discreet pathways between buildings until reaching the plain. A fair distance from the giant buildings and launch pads, I doubted I would be spotted out here.

Running, I scoured the rock-littered field searching for the entrance to the cave system. If the builders of this base had found it, they would have filled it, and I would have to take my chances at one of the main entrances. But since the openings of the buildings were all secured, I didn't imagine the mining areas were less so.

"Thank Hestra," I whispered when I found what I'd been looking for. A huge gray boulder half-buried under black and gray rocks obscured the wide opening. With one last look toward the base, I sat at the entrance and slid down the steep decline, tumbling rocks and gravel accompanying my descent.

Tapping my helmet light, I saw nothing had changed down here from when I explored it last.

Near the bottom of the slope, I stood and peered as far as my light shone into the tunnel. Although it had been a long time since my earlier explorations, it did not appear that those responsible for building the mining base had been in this cave tunnel.

Hastening my pace, I headed toward the caves that lay below the base. After being in her rooms, the woman's smell now saturated my systems; I could track her as soon as I found a trail of her atoms. But the Kezti, absent the ability to smell, had plenty of other abilities with which to hunt.

I ran faster, trusting my intuition to lead me close enough to any of her pathways that I might intercept her and prevent her capture by the Kezti.

Slowing as I approached a larger cavern, I saw dark recesses that lead to other tunnels. This far into the cave, I no longer recognized my surroundings. Standing at a juncture between two, I couldn't decide. And then I caught a whiff of rock dust, and something told me the rumble from before was the work of the survivor. Thankful for the clue, I chose the tunnel from which the dusty smell wafted.

Untouched, the tunnel's natural formation wasn't easily navigable. I hurried, but obstacles hedged up my path. Forced to step over fallen rocks or jump over large cracks, my nerves stretched taut. Would I find her in time?

The odor of spent material joined that of rock dust, and I knew I was drawing nearer. Squeezing through a narrow passage, I found myself in an open area. Not a cavern, but a large corridor with the look of having been hollowed by artificial means.

Before I could inspect it further, something powerful collided with the back of my helmet, and I saw a flurry of nebulae before my eyes. Shaking off the strike, I turned to face my attacker, but he struck me again, using the butt of his long-range weapon, much as I had done to his brother.

With colors bursting in my eyes and his first hit making my thoughts sluggish, I didn't deflect his second hit in time. I felt and heard the snap of my delicate calculut bone and roared in pain as my hand released hold of the gun I'd taken earlier. Twisting to protect the vulnerable side of my body, I grasped his weapon while he held it aloft for a third strike.

Driving it downward, I threw his balance off, kicked his leg and yanked the weapon out of his grip in one motion. While I had possession of his gun, he used my body to catch himself from falling, and we grappled. Strength for strength, we were well-matched. With my calculut bone broken, my entire right side was weak, but my kick had injured the Kezti's leg past its use.

Our grunts filled the dim corridor as we wrestled for dominance.

Chapter 7

Zooming in on the aliens in combat, I made out two distinct races. The praying mantis one, and the other with more humanoid features such as only two arms and a head attached to a neck wearing metallic armor and helmet. Lighting in the tunnel wasn't great; occasionally the light from the metallic armored being flashed into the camera.

Biting my lip, I tried to decide a proper course. I *knew* the bug aliens were here to kill me. From the harsh voice announcing the *Dynamo* was compromised, to the defenseless cave rat, to their methodical search across the planetoid, all evidence pointed to a fat target on my ass. However, they had no knowledge of the propulsion device, and if they found out about it, my career at IGMC was dead in the water. Not to mention how bad it could be for the human race if evil aliens decided to weaponize the Sphere Ship's engine.

The bug smashed his long gun into the other guy's arm so hard, his arm slackened, and his entire right side drooped.

Damn, that was a bad hit.

Pulling up the map, I traced a route with my finger. If I were to leave the dark tunnel, I could run to this guy's aid, presuming he was a good guy. That was the problem, though. I had no way of knowing. And leaving the engine room was tantamount to risking my career and my life.

Sweat poured down the back of my neck as I watched them wrestle each other. So far, they were evenly matched.

Beeping notified me of more motion on camera, and my gaze darted to the other monitors. As predicted, the aliens had found their way to the mining tunnels, but when met with my handcrafted redecorating, they were forced to follow tunnels that led back to the main cavern.

But there were only two wandering the tunnels.

One fighting the armored alien.

I needed to find the fourth. When the Victor left my apartment with the bug's weapon, I assumed the bug was dead. But what if it wasn't? I scrolled through the feeds, most of them looming over empty rooms or halls, some from surface buildings, every monitor showing the desolate operation, a ghost town now that its lifeblood, the humans, had left.

Scrolling feed after feed, I couldn't locate the fourth alien.

Checking to see the two were still headed away from Spoke Tunnel, I returned my attention to the battling aliens. A flash from the corner of the screen in an adjacent tunnel drew my gaze.

Damn. As I feared, he wasn't dead. In a few minutes he would come upon the two locked in combat and tip the scales.

I needed to decide now.

Leaving the inner sanctum was foolhardy. Reckless. Possibly stupid. Probably dangerous.

But I couldn't ignore the compulsion to help the alien wearing that shiny armor.

He hadn't started racing around until his altercation with one of the bugs. Was it possible he was trying to help? Or were the two species in a competition to capture the lone human on the planetoid?

Cursing again, I pressed fingers at my temples. If he'd incapacitated the bug at my apartment without killing him, maybe it was intentional. Maybe that meant a kind of honor code where he or his kind didn't go off indiscriminately killing people. Against my better judgment and every protocol written since the Sphere Ship blueprints were printed, I made my choice.

"DAPHNE, foolish or not, I'm about to leave the engine room and go help someone in trouble. Can you keep an eye on the fort?"

"Affirmative."

Running to the inner door, I activated the codes and sprinted down the dark tunnel. Once I exited into the Hub, I could take Tunnel Two. I knew where a branch forked off it. Yes, it would lead me down the same tunnel the fourth bug was in, but he wouldn't be expecting me.

Reaching the Hub, I made sure the door locked behind me and sprinted across the area to Two. Requiring only a thumbprint, the door slid open in seconds, and I raced, hoping I wouldn't be too late. Why was I doing this again?

Because of a hunch.

And every time I'd followed my hunch, something amazing had happened. I hoped with all my heart it would hold in this case, too.

Chapter 8

The Kezti was gaining the upper hand, as his two upper arms squeezed me around my shoulders and neck. Heh.

It wouldn't be long before he compromised my air vents and blood tunnel. A less humorous observation. Grunting with the effort, I used my good arm to encircle his narrow thorax and lift while simultaneously sliding my right leg behind his. Kicking back, I released his waist and shoved. As I'd hoped, his grip loosened as the sensation of falling triggered his four arms to windmill.

Drawing back my fist, I plowed a hit just under his chin, and he landed with a sprawl.

My gaze fell on the long-range weapon still gripped in one of his tight fists. He couldn't shoot me with it easily in here, but one more whack on my good arm, and it was all over.

With a desperate lunge, I dove for it, but he rolled toward it and protected it with his body as if it were a Kezti egg case. One of his fists pounded the break in my left arm, and I howled in pain.

Using my legs to pin his lower limbs, I twisted my torso to keep my bad arm out of reach and pounded against his shoulders and head, but his chitin protected him while bruising my knuckles. I needed a change of tactics. Not just that. My entire plan was circling a black hole. When the Kezti succeeded in crippling my efforts, he would join his brothers in finding the survivor and ending her life, treaties be damned.

I considered activating my comms, but to what end? Any warriors the Chak Dam Jai sent wouldn't get here in time to save the survivor or me. Leaning forward, I made a controlled fall and grasped the Kezti around its neck joint. Barely visible from even feet away, their neck joints articulated in two places. If I could edge my elbow between its jaw and upper body ...

It swung its weapon around and grabbing it with his other arms, he used it to crush against me, the force increasing by the moment. While my good arm was throttling his neck, he was crushing my lower back with the weapon, and I was useless to do anything to retaliate. My arm was too thick to get a proper grip because his jaw plates and upper body plates overlapped. Maybe—nebulae were circling my peripheral vision again—maybe the survivor could take care of herself. She had set off that explosion; I was almost certain.

Darkness clouded my vision, but I tried to work my arm closer.

A shot rang out in the small chamber, and the pressure on my back disappeared. Beneath me, the Kezti lay motionless. Disoriented, I stared at his eyes a span before realizing they were lifeless.

"Arryewohkay?" a voice spoke from behind us.

Scrambling off the Kezti's body, I groaned when the pain from my broken arm registered, the heat of battle no longer numbing its effects. I dropped to my knees and grimaced. When I raised my head to see who spoke, the survivor of the crashed shuttle stood at the cave's entrance with a smoking weapon. Breath caught in my throat; I stared at dark eyes the color of brownstone. Confusion muddled my vision, for it appeared her skin was flayed of all fur or scales in its smoothness and vulnerability. Like the tender skin at my throat. Likewise, her mouth lay flat under her nose, and I spied small, dull teeth. What was this person? Hating that the survivor's first impression of me was as a weak and injured victim, I further frowned upon realizing she was small of stature.

She said more words, but without a translator, I couldn't guess what she said. I squeezed my eyes shut as I inhaled slow, deep breaths. At last, my inhibitor glands released their chemical soup, and I exhaled and blinked, hand on my knee as I forced myself to stand.

The survivor stood in front of me, her hand reaching out to help, and her mouth gaping when I rose to my full height. Distance had fooled my eyes as well; I had imagined her larger when I spied her from my landing site.

When I leaned to pick up the Kezti's weapon, I shot a glance to the survivor, concerned she might feel threatened, but she gave me an approving smile and nodded at her own weapon.

It clicked into place; she had used her weapon to kill the Kezti. And then another thought eked its way between the mountain peaks of my pain.

She'd saved my life.

Gritting my teeth, I cursed. "Chamron falls."

I paused, staring, but her expression morphed into alarm, and she jabbed at her wrist, then beckoned for me to follow her. I left the second weapon behind; the long-range guns were unwieldy to begin with.

She slapped a helmet onto her head, and a light tracked the tunnel she entered. She sped through it, me close on her tail, as she dodged rocks, ancient gear, and an oozing Kezti corpse. Shocked, I stumbled but recovered before I fell. I wasn't entirely sure why she raced, but I thought she must have discovered she was being hunted, somehow knew I was in trouble, and subsequently, rescued me. She must have killed the other one first, and judging by its clotted wound, it was the one who'd found me in her apartment. *Falls.*

The survivor was thorough.

Several spans into the tunnel she slowed and gestured that we should be quiet. At least, that's what I thought she mimed. Her own movements had slowed, and she moved with the grace of a Dam Svai matalya, the jungle feline known for its stalking behavior.

Removing her helmet, she paused at an entrance and studied the cavern beyond.

Holding my broken arm to my side, I studied her.

I'd seen my share of curious travelers on the Causeway, but her species was a new one. Unless she was an aberration for her kind, they fell on the small end of the spectrum. With no visible protrusions such as spikes or ridges, her skin seemed a liability, but she did have filaments covering her head and tied into a knot at the base of her neck. Likewise, she had no tail, wings, clubs, talons, claws or spikes. A wholly unprotected species with no outward signs of defense.

And yet.

She'd killed two Kezti and saved my life.

Perhaps her race made up in intelligence and strategy, cleverness and cunning, where their bodies lacked strength or armor.

She waved me forward, and we ventured into the cavern. A quick glance revealed much had been done in the several revolts since last I explored here. She jogged to a huge pile of rubble, and I wondered if we'd have to scale it when she disappeared before my eyes.

Blinking, I wiped my eyes, but she was still gone. I circled, ignoring the dull ache in my arm, but saw nowhere she could have gone. She popped out from behind the rubble and waved again, and I followed, understanding dawning on me as I rounded the pile. It had spilled in such a way as to create an optical illusion. She crouched down and crawled into a dark square; I doubted my ability to fit but she moved with such purpose I had to try.

Gasping when my arm caught the edge, I swallowed the groan lodged in my throat as I forced myself through the small passage. Once through the space, we stood and raced down a long tunnel. Now my arm throbbed with every footfall and dizzying shapes circled my vision, but I kept the survivor in focus.

At the end of the tunnel, she granted us access into an incredible spacious room filled with computers. I watched her jog to a non-descript doorway and stop. She waited for me, her expression calm. It seemed we neared her destination. She had stopped checking her wrist once we reached the huge empty cavern.

A recess hid to the left of the doorway, and she turned into it, making sure I followed.

She turned on her headlamp again, and we jogged the distance to another door. She held her hand out for me to wait while she stood on a black rectangle and performed a similar ritual to the one she'd done earlier today to enter her building of apartments. The door slid open after several lights danced in a pattern on a screen to the right, and she beckoned me to enter.

The door slid shut behind us and she stood at a panel and pushed an array of buttons. A computerized voice made an announcement, and she turned to face the room, letting her head fall against the door and helmet clatter to the side as she slid all the way down with a gusty sigh.

Surprised at this show of vulnerability, I turned away, wishing to give her a moment of privacy. I took the opportunity to walk around the room that five or six of my ships could easily fit into. A large bank of machines and screens filled a half-circle in the center. Surrounding that command center were more machines and chairs, but everything appeared to be arrayed to face a blank metal wall.

At the perimeter of the circular room, several doors stood closed. I was curious, but not rude enough to begin exploring when I'd not been invited to do so.

Beeping emitted from one of the screens in the command center and I approached. Rows upon rows of smaller screens showed video footage of a myriad of places on Hestra's Handmaid. That's how the survivor found me!

A flashing light blinked in rhythm to the beeping noise on one screen, and I saw the two remaining Kezti warriors running through a huge hall. Movement at my side indicated the survivor approached. I stepped aside to give her access, and she said a few quiet words and shook her head.

She leaned on the console and watched the Kezti run down a corridor, disappear, and then reappear on a separate screen. They appeared to be studying the walls with care, and I surmised she worried they would find the cleverly concealed entryway. Considering the tight fit it had been for me, I doubted a Kezti would even try to contort itself, but then again, they could be a stubborn bunch. Yet, the doorways we'd entered had been secure, and the last path obscured. I recalled the hub we'd first entered had several doors ringing it. Even if they could open each one, they'd have to run all the way down the tunnels and try to access whatever door was at the end.

Knowing the Kezti, I predicted they would give up in three more spans.

Cradling my arm, I watched the screens with her until she turned and stared at me, a deep groove forming in her skin above her eyes. Her flat teeth bit on her lower lip and she cocked her head. Unintelligible words spilled from her mouth, and she ran to one of the white doors. It slid open; she turned and motioned I should come.

Once inside the room, the bright light hurt my eyes even through my helmet, and I held my hand over the visor.

I heard drawers opening and metallic instruments clatter onto a tray. Blinking away the moisture that gathered in my eyes, I struggled to remove my helmet one-handed. I smelled her before I sensed her nearness, a hint of lama fruit and something else pleasant but unrecognizable, but my eyes were closed as I tried to take off the helmet. She attempted to help, but I waved her hands away and resigned myself to leaving it on for now.

She smiled and patted a large chair.

Scowling, I stared at it. Instead of sitting, I stalked to where she stood and looked at the tray that held the sharp instruments I'd heard when the light blinded me.

"What are you intending to do to me, Survivor?" I said and flicked at one of the tools until it spun in place.

I knew she couldn't understand me, but a soft smile touched her lips and she gestured to my broken arm. Doubting she had the ability or understanding to heal my physiology, I rolled my shoulders. It was a gesture my people understood as 'no', 'leave me alone', or 'I disagree', but she cocked her head, and that groove appeared on her head skin again.

Frowning, she crossed one arm over her chest and tapped her lip with the finger of her other one.

"Fallohmee," she said and left the room, though she left the light on and the door open. I followed her again, curious.

She led me to the screen array and manipulated some levers and dials. She pointed to a screen, and I saw the battle between the Kezti and I. Wincing at the moment he smashed his weapon into my arm, she turned to me and touched my chest armor. Her expression bore concern and she pointed at my arm again.

It was clear she desired to attempt to heal it, but she couldn't know of my doubts until I showed her.

"Very well," I said, though she couldn't know my meaning. I returned to the medical room on my own, and I heard her pleased sigh from behind. "You'll find out soon enough this will never work," I grumbled. Before I sat in the chair, I removed my armor, stacking it on the floor nearby.

As much pain as radiated from the break into the rest of my body, I couldn't help the laugh that erupted from my belly when I saw the look on her face. How could a race of soft-skins comprehend the Dam Svai? My laughter trailed off as I let my broken arm rest in my lap. I supposed I had better let her try, anyway. Perhaps her peculiarly weak race had mastered the art of pain management, considering they had no way to prevent injuries from the slightest contact. Sneaking peeks at her bare hands, I had already spied numerous scars as well as scrapes and bruises.

Hestra's Hells, I could snap her in two with a brutal sneeze.

Sighing, I made myself comfortable and waited to see what she would do next.

Chapter 9

I'd called him humanoid in my mind. Compared to the praying Mantis aliens, he was far closer to my own physiognomy—with his armor and helmet on.

But even though I'd obscured my gasp of surprise, I couldn't hide the astonishment that must be evident on my face as his helmet and armor sat beside the chair and he turned to look at me.

The armored warrior who I suspected and hoped had planned to help me, was, in truth, reptilian.

He didn't have a long snout like the reptiles on Jeppsit 5, but his facial structure was definitely rounded at his nose and mouth where my mouth and face would be considered flat to him. His face wasn't the most surprising feature.

The scales on his shoulders I'd thought were part of his armor were in fact, protruding from his skin. And his scaled skin bore several bumpy ridges along the outer edge where his elbows bent outward.

A guttural eruption broke forth from the Victor, and I couldn't be sure, but I thought maybe he was laughing at me. Clearing my throat, I composed my features, fearing I'd been unforgivably rude, and found the portable X-ray unit. Flexible and thin, I could slide it with care underneath his broken arm and fold it over the top. With the press of a button, the irradiated image appeared on the nearest screen.

My frown deepened. No wonder he groaned when he squeezed into the egress chute. The weapon had shattered the bone above his joint. I stared and covered my mouth. I wasn't trained to do much aside from administer basic first aid and pain meds.

"Well, shit," I finally said out loud. Shaking my head, I replaced the instruments I thought I'd need to remove fabric, like a sleeve. But he wasn't wearing any kind of under armor shirt. Just his incredibly sturdy scales that protected his arms with its thick layer. The scales smoothed out to sleeker rounded shapes across his chest and abdomen, somehow delineating every ripped muscle. Tearing my eyes away, I opened cupboard doors until I found the small cache of pain management drugs. Would they even work with his physiology? For his sake, I hoped so.

Turning to face him, I caught him staring at me, his head cocked, and brow ridges furrowed.

This would be easier with translation, of course.

"Computer, can you adapt the translation software used in the comms towers down here?" I asked.

"Of course," she said. "Please have communicant speak."

Carrying a couple different pain management options closer to where the Victor sat, I held them in my hand and then pointed to his broken arm. "Would you like to try any of these?" The computer needed a sampling from Victor, so I hoped he would respond.

"Unless your medicines are comprised of topical oils harvested from the forests of Mother Dam, they won't work," the computer overlaid Victor's gravelly voice.

"But shouldn't we at least try?" I asked.

His brow ridges lifted.

"We have means to communicate, now?" he said, his surprise evident.

"Yes," I said with a smile. "I'm Shay Leviticus. Can't we do something for your arm?"

He scowled. "It's the calculut bone. Why the Mother Dam gave us these fragile bones that grow beside the main bone makes no sense." He looked me up and down. "Shay Leviticus? I am Drail."

Smiling again, I nodded to see if he would say more, but he didn't.

"But the medicine?" I said and gestured.

"How is it administered?" he said with resignation.

Fishing through the jumble of bottles, I realized most of them required injection. I pulled a syringe out of the designated drawer but didn't remove the sterile wrap yet.

"May I see your arm?" I said and stood beside the chair.

Standing this close, I lost myself in his presence for a few seconds, overwhelmed by his size, his otherness, his scent, and I gripped the nearby countertop to steady myself.

Until now, I hadn't studied his face or skin with scrutiny, but under the guise of trying to help, I devoured his details with as much alacrity as I could, not wishing to be obvious. Our time together would likely be short.

With brief glances at his face, I noticed his thick brow ridges overshadowing intelligent, bright green eyes. The skin around his eyes was smooth rather than scaly but the rough, spiked skin on his arms, shoulders, neck, and back appeared impenetrable. No way a syringe was getting through that.

"You can touch it," he said, his voice low and rumbly.

Hot blood infused my cheeks, though I knew he was referring to his forearm, the uninjured part. I demurred, but he grasped my hand with his good one and placed it on the back of his other.

"Brush upward and see how the texture changes," he said.

Peeking at his eyes, I saw them narrow when he looked at me, and the corner of his vicious smile turned up, revealing dangerous teeth.

I averted my gaze and let my fingers drift from the cool bumpiness on the back of his huge, clawed hand up his arm to where scales were more pronounced. The break was past his elbow, so I stopped there, but noticed how the scales thickened the farther up his arm they went until the prominent ones at his shoulders stood proudly.

When I checked his expression again, he grinned, smug.

"You see your brittle, insignificant needles would break upon the skin of the Dam Svai," he said, his smile defiant.

His green eyes watched me, as if he were waiting for my response.

Studying his face, I looked for a crack in his sardonic armor. With thin lips that slipped up when he spoke, his superiority complex persisted. The rough texture of his skin shifted with every word, and bumpy brow ridges revealed facile movement: proof he could vary his expression from something other than haughtiness if he chose. The smoother skin around his eyes and on his cheeks thickened around his nose and mouth, then smoothed out again under his chin and on his throat. It might be the only place on his body vulnerable to a strike.

"Hoom," he said again, and I realized it was a vocal tic he used when he was thinking. "I would ask you a question because I lack understanding."

Wrinkling my nose, I cocked my head.

He raised his good hand and hovered it near my hand, quirking a brow. I gave him a slow nod and watched with interest when he used his index finger to caress the skin on the back of my hand with gentle strokes. "I do not understand why a creator would design their children with defenseless skin," he said. "What are these various wounds from?"

He touched the scratches and scars that littered my hands. His touch sent sparks deep in my gut, and I caught myself on the brink of panting. I exhaled. It had been a long time since I had been touched gently like ... that. I swallowed and cleared my throat.

"From my work in the mines," I said. "I'm always scraping against rock or tools. I have gloves I could wear, but they make my hands sweat inside. I work with explosives, so I'm picky about how my hands feel. It's better if I have full dexterity."

"Mining seems a treacherous livelihood for ones with so few defenses," he said with a sneer and took my hand, pressing the ends of my fingers where my nails barely reached my fingertips. "How is it you overpowered not one, but two Kezti pirates this day?" He sounded disgruntled about it, but I chalked it up to wounded male pride.

Patting my sidearm, I shrugged. "I had an unfair advantage. Let's leave it at that."

He scowled and pushed himself out of the chair so he now towered above me.

"Mayhap your creator was foolish to craft a weak race, but mine is no wiser," he said and walked out.

Confused at his irritation, I looked down at my scraped-up hands. He hadn't said anything specific about his goddess that made her sound unwise to my ears, other than the remark about his *calculut* bone.

I caught up to him. "Why are these Kezti called pirates?" I said.

"Ah, the Kezti warriors," he said with a moue of distaste. "My people, the Dam Svai, consider them to be wastrels and pirates because they trawl the Causeway for stranded or isolated ships and pillage for their own gain."

"Causeway?" I asked

"I judge you are unfamiliar with Chamron's star system?" he asked and gestured upward. I assumed he called WD-237 Chamron.

"Only familiar enough to know that in a few days' time, this planet will be frozen solid, along with everything and everyone on it."

He sighed. "That is the other matter we must speak of," he said, his gaze slanting away from my face for a moment. "Chamron marks one of the outer reaches of my people's jurisdiction. We patrol the Causeway, a busy space corridor through which many races travel to engage in trade and leisure."

I grabbed a nearby stool and sat. "We had no idea," I said.

He smiled; at least I thought the upturned corners of his toothy mouth signified that.

"No, you did not," he said. "But no matter. The Dam Svai welcome all peoples to use the Causeway to increase economies. Had your ship stumbled across it, the Causeway Passage Authority would have requested an introduction and provided a security detail. It is our goal to prevent these such ... circumstances," he said and gestured all around.

"Like the Kezti compromising the *Dynamo,* the mother ship," I said.

He sighed. "Yes and destroying the communications halfway point."

"Oh god," I said and covered my eyes. Marsel Granda *was* dead. It was just as I'd feared.

"My condolences," Drail said with a bob of his head. "If it offers consolation, my people will have restored your *Dynamo* to its proper command by now and sent the Kezti war ships running with their tails between their legs."

I didn't recall seeing tails on the monster alien bugs but I appreciated the computer's efforts to translate cultural idioms. Or maybe the Dam Svai had tails?

"So, if I could get off this planet, I could return to the *Dynamo* safely?" I asked.

"Yes, I'm happy to inform you of this," he said with another dangerous smile.

Beeping from the main computer drew our attention, and I gave him a reluctant smile. "I need to check this, sorry."

He bobbed his head and I hurried to the monitors.

"Wastrels and pirates, huh?" I said and cursed, wishing I could punch something. Drail appeared beside me, silent for one his size.

"They destroyed your communication towers," he observed with no emotion in his voice.

"Yes, they destroyed every last one of them, dammit," I said. Monitors showed all three smoking where they stood, victims of a weaponry I hadn't seen the Kezti use. I only spotted them as they ran to their ship. Then they separated and each took a flyer.

If what my new friend said was accurate, Captain Mear would be reinstated and losing his mind right about now. He would have taken roll call and discovered Granda's and my absence.

"If the Captain knew I was here, he could just send one of the shuttles back," I said to myself. The Kezti ships fired and took off, flying low over the dormitory building and releasing what looked like a slow-moving dark gray bowling ball.

"Get down!" Drail shouted and tackled me, landing us both on the smooth poured-cement floor. From my angle by the rolling office chair, I could just make out a huge black cloudburst on the monitor about two seconds before the floor shuddered and the monitors rattled at their stations. Otherwise, all was well. This was a mining base, after all, accustomed to concussive blasts of all kinds.

We groaned as we pulled to standing, Drail's grimace ugly in its pain.

"Do you have any pain medicine with you?" I asked. My thoughts raced. "Or on your ship?"

"I do not travel with much by way of medicine, little Survivor," he said. "And I would happily escort you back to your *Dynamo*, but sadly, my ship only supports a single occupant."

"Of course, it does," I said to myself and bit my lip, fisting my hands at my waist and pacing. "Those Kezti bastards split up and took both ships they came with and blew out the towers. Unless my captain thinks to come looking for me, he may assume I'm dead."

Cursing, I paced around the computer banks and spared a quick glance at the wall that concealed the planet propulsion device. Sworn to secrecy, I couldn't let Drail know what was behind the wall.

Sighing, I stopped my mad walking and faced him as he stood observing me without comment.

"What do we do now?" I asked. Glancing at the monitors, the smoking debris signaled one more event in the hell-spiral my day had taken.

"I should have explained earlier that I am capable of communicating with my superior from my helmet," Drail said. "I will inform him you are in need of transport back to your ship."

"Thank god," I said and collapsed into the nearest chair.

He returned to the med bay where his gear was, and I watched his powerful stride. The praying mantis aliens were also huge, but their legs and arms were stalks as opposed to musculature formed over bones. When I'd snuck up behind the one in the tunnel, I'd let second thoughts paralyze me. But it must have heard my grippers displace a pebble because it'd spun and swung its arms at me. Two shots killed it, but where I might have spared regret, its hideous barbed dagger dropped from one of its arms, and my worries stilled.

Seeing Drail slump once I had found the chamber where he wrestled with the other bug hardened my resolve, and my second kill had taken no thought.

My new alien companion remained composed in spite of horrific pain, respected my personal space and offered to get me a ride off MP-13, where the other warriors had had much more violent intentions where I was concerned.

Drail exited the med bay with his helmet in place, and I knew I'd made the right decision.

Chapter 10

My debt-mate wore a satisfied expression when I returned to her command center. I had questions but resigned myself to quiet observation until we knew more about each other. However, I owed her my life and anything within my power to give, as the Dam Svai Code demanded, so I hailed my superior, even as she watched from her chair. I noted with curiosity it rolled on wheels but did not remark on it. What a strange race.

"Chak Dam Jai," I said. "I found the survivor. She needs transport to her mother ship. Will you inform her captain? The survivor's base communications are down; the Kezti took out their comms waystation, as well."

"Please standby," he said. "We may have stumbled upon a bit of a—complication."

Furrowing my brow, I cocked my head. "In what way?"

"Standby."

Confused, I watched Shay's expressive face. Doubtless her translator had translated my side of the conversation; her brow was likewise creased in consternation, though she would not know what my superior said.

"Hoom," I said, nodding to her. "Only a moment."

Her shoulders tensed.

Crackling in my helmet drew my attention.

"When we restored command to the *Dynamo*, all was well," the Chak Dam Jai said. "But as we forcibly removed the Kezti pirates, one of them started shouting about being double-crossed."

"I see," I said, and turned my back on Shay. She could not see my face through my helmet anyway, but a slither of doubt uncurled at the base of my spine.

"Naturally, this caused questions to arise on both sides," he said. "The *Dynamo's* captain, and myself."

"And what have you found?" I asked, my voice calm, though my insides trembled. Why *was* Shay Leviticus here, a woman alone, on the abandoned planetoid? Why was she not with others? What was this finely appointed command center in the bowels of Hestra's Handmaid, in which nothing resembled the coarse utilitarian buildings of an established mining base?

I noticed how her gaze drifted to the blank wall when she thought I wasn't watching. Claws trailing the gleaming console, I observed how each item shone from diligent upkeep.

Monitors and systems that appeared of an equivalent or superior technology to the Dam Svai, pristine walls and floors, luxurious fabric on the chairs and lighting perfectly balanced over each workstation. Not to mention the lack of damage felt in spite of the Kezti dropping one of their most powerful bombs.

Double and triple security measures.

Fearing what I might see on Shay's features, I refused to turn back yet. Had this courageous woman, my very debt-mate, betrayed her own people? Perhaps in relation to this secret chamber deep within the rocky planetoid?

My mind raced at the possibilities and relentlessly returned to the blank wall.

"We've separated the Kezti pirate from the others as well as *Dynamo's* captain," the Chak Dam said. "I advise caution until we know more, Drail."

Clearing my throat, I scratched at my armor over my chest and turned to Shay Leviticus. "There is a delicate matter I must discuss with my superior," I said. "Could you be so kind as to request the translator to refrain for a few moments?"

"Of course," Shay said without hesitation.

Her technology's voice entered my helmet. "Translation paused."

Shay offered me a smile and then gestured to a door as she approached it. When it opened, I glimpsed what resembled a hygiene facility inside, and I relaxed.

"Chak Dam Jai," I said. "The survivor killed two of the Kezti pirates."

"That lessens her likelihood in involvement, doesn't it?" the Chak Dam said.

"Hoom. Well. She killed them in order to save my life," I said.

Silence for a beat.

"She is your debt-mate," he said.

"Aye."

"Chamron falls," he said. "This does put a jagged rock under the wheel."

"If comms drop," I said, and took a deep breath. "You'll know why."

"Indeed, Drail," he said. "Until then, I'll keep you abreast."

"Thank you."

"Sound blessings, Drail," he said.

"And bright stars," I said, closing our connection.

Cracking my neck, I rolled my shoulders and removed my helmet, wincing when I jostled my bad arm. Shay exited a moment later and tossed me a half-smile.

"Everything alright?" she said. "Captain Mear should be able to spare one of the remaining shuttles, I would think. Assuming your people were able to regain control of the ship."

While her demeanor was confident, her voice wavered. Stalking close to her, I traced the air around her head with my snout. Yes, I smelled fear and that elusive floral note reminiscent of lama fruit, but also bravery and resolution. My debt-mate was a stubborn one. She didn't flinch away, even though I suspected her own people seldom used their scenting protuberances as mine did. Hers was small, and just like her teeth, ineffectual.

"There is no question that the Dam Svai wrenched control from the grasping, greedy claws of the Kezti pirates," I said and brought my claw up to touch her chin. The smoothness of her skin beguiled me, though this was no time nor place to marvel at such things. I cupped her chin, and she caught her breath. "One of the pirates claims he worked in tandem with one of your people, to what end, I do not know." My grip tightened a fraction before I let go.

Shay's eyes darkened and her nostrils flared. Heat wafted from her skin, and I stepped back a pace in surprise. My own people's skin did not radiate heat in this way.

"Are you insinuating I had a hand in Captain Mear's ship being attacked? And my own shuttle being shot down—while I was *in* it?"

Shay's voice was a band of metal, tightening around my chest. She continued. "And did I sic those Kezti dogs on you so I could manufacture a story for your benefit?"

Motioning with my hands that she should calm down, I spoke.

"Calm yourself, debt-mate," I said.

A tidal wave of heat crashed against me; I felt it rise from her face and neck. Once more, I was forced to create distance between us.

"Calm myself?" she said in a voice resembling a growl. "I have busted my ass for IGMC for the last ten years of my life." Her voice measured and soft, I harbored a suspicion that she masked fury. The heat of her anger could almost sear my skin. But she behaved as if we were discussing news while sipping hot damjest during the morning meal. I was not fooled and kept my distance, though an itch in my fingers bade me touch her face again.

"I don't know if it is you, or your superior, or some kind of fucking mistranslation between your superior and my captain, but my loyalty has never been questioned, not even once," she said. "Could you be so kind as to patch my computer into your superior so we can clear this up? It's not that long before everything on MP-13 is going to freeze solid, and if I'm not off this asphalt snow cone, I'll be covered in a four-inch layer of ice, too."

Resisting the urge to pat the air once more with my hands, I bobbed my head.

"Hoom. Your every request is my honor and duty," I said and bowed, though the words curdled in my mouth. She spoke the very doubts found within my thoughts. Was this sorcery of some kind? "I only await more news from my Dam Jai."

Mollified, Shay folded her arms across her chest, and I admired where her curves rose and dipped with her indignance. But fiery hot anger flared in my belly, and I turned away again, questioning Svai's Design.

The debt-mate Code hearkened to ancient times, when survival depended on social contracts within a community. To save another's life was to incur their lifelong servitude, until one's service had been fulfilled, or until the debt-mate returned the favor.

The Kezti had almost killed me.

Now I must serve Shay Leviticus for the rest of her life, or I supposed, save it. Stilling my fierce thoughts, I considered my debt may be quickly discharged once I secured her safe passage off Handmaid.

Giving her a side glance, I turned to face the blank wall and stood with my hands clasped behind my back. I wondered if it would make her uncomfortable to face it, and I noted with inner glee that it did.

I detected pinkness creeping up her cheeks, and she fidgeted with her hands, twisting them together while she worried dry skin from her lip with her teeth.

Frowning, I stared at the wall. What was she hiding?

Chapter 11

Thoughts raced while the huge reptilian alien stared at the wall concealing my magnum opus. I didn't like it, but I needed to restrain myself from trying to draw his attention away. Besides, there was more going on.

By Drail's account, the Kezti were a bunch of criminals. Why would one rogue alien shouting about being double-crossed suddenly make his leader, the Dam Svai, suspicious? And Captain Mear had to know I've laid down my life for the Sphere Ship. *Nothing* would convince me to sell the technology. And Marsel Granda was dead. Unless the Captain himself had somehow ... It made no sense. None of us knew about Drail's Causeway or anything this far out. Hell, even if we wanted to sell the tech, as far as we knew, there was no one to sell it to in this space backwater.

And the cost? My planet engine was priceless.

IGMC knew it, and that's why they'd been willing to sign all the contracts promising me and my future descendants countless wealth upon delivery. They were in my debt if this thing worked as promised.

Speaking of debt, something Drail said earlier popped back to mind. *Calm yourself, debt-mate.* I'd been so incensed that I didn't even process the following phrase. Debt-mate? Biting my lip, I frowned. Cross-cultural translation was fascinating as well as laborious. The computer would have chosen the closest possible match to Drail's meaning and provided the words in my language.

"Drail," I said, succeeding in bringing his attention back to me and away from the wall, thank god. "What did you mean when you addressed me as 'debt-mate'?"

I thought he scowled before; his entire demeanor turned into a grimace.

"You saved my life," he said, rolling his shoulders as he did so. "I am bound by Svai's Design and the Code of Debt to serve you until my debt is paid. But who can put a price on a life?" His brow ridges angled and then bunched again. "My debt to you can never be paid unless I save your life in like manner."

His expression was so dour I realized why he'd become irritable earlier. He was unhappy with the turn of events but powerless to change them unless he denied his own people's tradition.

"Well, I couldn't stand here and do nothing," I said and turned away, feeling my face heat. "I saw you fighting, and when he smashed your arm with that gun .... But I knew that other Kezti was on his way." I shuddered. Rubbing both of my arms, I remembered Drail's graphic X-ray. "What are we going to do about that, anyway?" I asked and approached him, putting my own discomfort out of my mind for now.

"It will knit on its own," he said.

"You're kidding me. You saw the X-ray. The end of that bone is *shattered*," I said.

"It is," he said. "Believe me when I say I can feel each and every shard as it gravitates to its mother-bone."

I imagined the sharp bone fragments migrating through his tissue. I tasted bile.

"You look like you swallowed a boll beetle," he said with amusement. "But please do not trouble yourself over it. Only two revolts past, my friend Alion was trampled by a rock beast. It broke his leg in two places, but now he competes in the Lekshi Games. All will be well," he said with a grim laugh. Noting my furrowed brow, he stepped closer and touched my temple with his good hand. "I'm duty-bound to ease your discomfort. If my pain distresses you so, perhaps you could fashion a sling for me to wear? It may lessen the pain I feel."

Relieved at his suggestion and alarmed by the jolt I felt at his touch, I pulled away and hurried to the bay. "I have something."

When I pulled the sling out of its storage cubby, I stared at it. It was designed for human arms and would never work for the much larger Drail. My gaze drifted to the bandage drawer. It wasn't an official sling, but it was long enough that it would work. I pulled out the roll of thick bandaging and found Drail outside the door waiting for me. He stood patiently while I wound it from under his arm and over his opposite shoulder, then around again and over the same shoulder. I fastened the clip to hold it in place. It would do.

"Thank you, debt-mate," he said, his voice soft.

I huffed out a humorless laugh. "We need to clear this up right now," I said. "In my language, 'mate' means, like, a permanent partner. The way my computer is translating your word is 'debt-mate', which makes it sound like you're in debt to me, and therefore I own you as a result." I shook my head. "That doesn't sound right. It makes it sound like we're *bonded* as life partners." I let out a short laugh. "Just because I saved your life."

Drail stood silent, letting his gaze trace my heated face and furrowed brow.

"Your computer has translated it correctly," he said, a deep groove furrowing his brow.

Tunnel vision filtered out the entire room, and I felt my face go white. All I could see was Drail and his glowering expression. Standing there huge and strong with his menacing scales and protruding mouth and nose forming a short snout, exuding power but also a sense of ... dismay.

If possible, he liked the prospect even less than I did.

Pinching the bridge of my nose, I closed my eyes and took a deep breath. Releasing both, I rested my hands at my hips.

"I respect that your culture is different and that you possess lifetimes of unique codes and mores and traditions," I said. "But that doesn't mean I have to embrace it, okay?"

He said nothing; his frown only deepened.

"I release you from the debt," I said with a flourish and wave of my hands. "How about that?"

He rolled his shoulders again and stared at me.

"The Code of Debt only requires that I abide by it," he said. "If you already have a mate, you keep them. If I somehow do not repay you on this planet, I go where you go, always a protector at your side. Your wishes, desires and demands will be mine, and I will perform all in my power to grant them."

Cocking my head, I stepped closer and peered into his beautiful, intelligent green eyes with the vertical slit pupil, trying to divine his thoughts. The words he said were poignant, powerful, and yet the emotion behind them was so empty. He was miserable.

"But you don't want this anymore than I do," I said. "We're from different worlds. My occupation takes me across galaxies. You'd have to leave everything you know behind."

"I know this, woman!" he barked.

Startled, I took a step back. "I don't understand why you can't just refuse the Code," I said and folded my arms.

He approached me and reached out his good arm. Grasping me around my bicep, his hand encircled it.

"It is true, this is not something I asked for," he said. He dipped his head. "I apologize for the artless way I've expressed my duty, for you are correct. I will necessarily leave my entire life behind to follow you and fulfill the Code. My emotions are ... powerful." He stopped and licked his lips with a smooth black tongue, and I stared, transfixed. "I leave my other responsibilities behind. And my friends. But if I were to abandon this duty, then my people would abandon me."

The permanence of it stunned me, and I had to retreat from him, find a chair and sit. I leaned forward, elbows on my knees, and held my head in my hands.

"This isn't right," I said. I heard soft footfalls as he approached and stood nearby.

"Forgive me," he said, and I felt his hand dip beneath my chin, and he lifted it so my gaze met his. "I've gone about it all wrong."

He knelt in front of me so we could meet at eye level.

"You have my deepest gratitude," he said. "I should not have forgotten the magnitude of your gift to me. A life for a life."

Cheeks burning, I swallowed. "I would do it again," I said. "I watched the Kezti when they disembarked. Shooting up equipment and killing innocent animals," I said. "I knew they would harm me. I wasn't certain, but I thought you meant me no harm. It was a calculated risk."

Tilting his head, he blinked, his eyelids moving vertically.

"You're brave considering your woeful lack of reliable defenses," he said.

I shook my head. "Humans have plenty of defenses," I said. "Innovative weapons chiefly among them." I touched my sidearm. "I really don't understand this Code of Debt. What if I saved several of you at once? Would you all follow me around? What if you were someone else's debt-mate? Would that cancel out the first one?"

Drail scratched his brow ridge and sighed.

"Such vagaries have assorted protocols, but this instance is quite clear," he said. "And had I not informed my superior of my debt to you, and he found out via other means, I would be harshly reprimanded and stripped of my ranks and appointments."

Sitting back in my chair, I groaned and covered my eyes against the ceiling lights. "That was the delicate matter," I said.

"Yes."

Rubbing my eyes, I suddenly felt very tired. "Well then," I said. "First things first. We need to get off planet sometime in the next six days, preferably this one. Then we can worry about this mate business." I lowered my gaze to meet Drail's, and his expression relaxed.

"It may be that successfully returning you to your people could qualify as debt payment," he said and bobbed his head with an accompanying 'hoom'.

Huffing a laugh, I stood and stretched. "See? We were worried for nothing. Did your superior say how long before he'd know something?"

A strange light sparked in Drail's eyes, but he averted his gaze and stood in a fluid motion, his injured arm safely tucked into his side.

"He did not, but it should not be too much longer," he said.

"Wake me as soon as you hear," I said and walked to another set of doors. "Take the other room if you like; I have to sleep. I've been up eighteen hours."

The weight of the day's activities bore down on my shoulders, and I collapsed onto the narrow bed with relief. The planet engine was locked up tight with my security measures, and the AGI wouldn't allow Drail to do any snooping on the computers. And if I was honest, I felt safe with him around, even though I was the one who'd rescued his grumpy ass. Life could be weird.

Chapter 12

Dark circles under her eyes, Shay summarily dismissed me, and she closed the door behind her. In truth, it had been a busy day even before I landed on Handmaid.

Subsequent events had been stressful and tiresome. It was a pity my recon ship only sat one. While my debt-mate was courageous and intelligent, wily and compassionate, I could not envision spending longer than a few rotations with her. Would she belabor every point when I tried to explain our ways?

Walking to the blank wall, I touched it and felt a thrumming power through the metal. Scrutinizing it with eyes and hands, I sought a seam but found none. For now, whatever pulsed behind the wall would remain a mystery.

"Chak Dam Jai," I said in my comms. "What have you learned?"

"Standby, Drail," he said, his voice solemn.

The Code of Debt was an ancient law that superseded all others in my people's government. Should it be discovered that Shay Leviticus betrayed her Captain and people by working with the Kezti, I still remained at her side, and my duty remained as well: to protect and serve her. It would become my work to help her evade her own people's administration of justice.

Spying the curious chair with wheels, I sat on it, and it rolled a few strets on the smooth floor, throwing me off balance. Holding out my arms, I steadied the roll until it stopped. I planted my boots on the floor and stared at the blank wall, waiting to hear what my Chak Dam Jai had to say.

"Drail," he said a few moments later. "The rogue Kezti reported a woman promised him boundless wealth if they attacked the *Dynamo* creating a diversion so she may take control of the mining base."

"*Falls,*" I uttered.

"Her captain has declared her a traitor and sends a team to extract and arrest her now," he said. He was silent a bit and then continued. "You know what you must do."

"*Chamron falls,*" I said and made fists.

"It has been a pleasure and an honor, Drail, Son of Madhera. Serve your debt with honor."

"Sound blessings," I said, my voice hoarse.

"And bright stars," the Chak Dam Jai said.

Turning to face the door behind which Shay Leviticus slept, my peripheral vision caught movement at the same moment beeping chimed from the computing systems.

I watched a monitor on which could be seen a Kezti vanguard ship landing on one of the shuttle docks.

Leaning on the console with both hands, I shouted for Shay.

"Hasten to me, Woman!"

Shay Leviticus appeared at her door, hair awry, and saw me at the large monitor. She strode to where I stood, and we watched together as four more Kezti pirates exited their ship. And a fifth, smaller person of Shay's race.

"Marsel fucking Granda," she said, her voice ice cold, though my skin sensed her rising temperature where she stood beside me.

"My Chak Dam Jai informed me that your captain is sending a team to arrest you," I said. "This does not appear to be the extraction team."

With darkened eyes and flushed cheeks, she pointed at the screen.

"You're right. That is no extraction team," she said, her voice low and thick. "I've been set up."

Staring at her, this being of seductive smoothness and delicate structures, I saw not a weak female, but a wrathful warrior prepared to wreak vengeance on her enemies.

"My debt to you stands," I said, my own voice husky with emotion. "I am your servant in this and in all things. What would you have me do?"

For a second, her expression softened, and I saw her swallow, judging by a movement in her neck. Then her eyes narrowed, and her resolve returned.

"Let me show you something," she said and jogged to the wall where the lighting controls were. She punched at its surface and spoke. "You're serious about this debt-mate business?"

I nodded and brought my fist to my chest.

"Then you're sworn to secrecy."

"Of course," I answered but then heard a swishing sound behind me. The lights dimmed as the metal wall slid apart to reveal a huge cell cast in a blue glow. At its center floated a metal construction that rotated at a slow rate; it was a hollow cube set within a larger hollow cube. I didn't hear Shay come up behind me until she spoke at my side.

"This is a planet engine," she said. "I designed and built it for IGMC." She rested a small hand on the clear barrier between the control room and the cell. "It's my life's work, and my colleague is coming to get it."

"The small man with the Kezti pirates," I clarified.

"Yes."

Hypnotized by the pulse of energy I couldn't hope to understand, I pulled my gaze away.

"Of course, we must defend it," I said.

When she turned to face me, she blinked back liquid forming in her eyes. "If I die, destroy it. If they get it before I die, kill me."

Taken aback, I searched her face for misgivings but found none. I gave her a single nod.

She ran to the monitors. Reaching for her helmet sitting on the desk, she snapped it on.

"Captain Mear's extraction team should arrive in about—"

"Drail, Kezti's entire force just blinked outside Hestra's atmosphere," the Dam Jai's voice alerted me. "Captain Mear's extraction team ship was blown apart. We are at war."

"Chamron falls," I said through gritted teeth. "Woman, the Kezti have declared war upon your people and the Dam Svai. Your mining planet will be under attack in mere spans. What are your orders?"

Shay was at the entrance of the engine room unpacking a bag.

"Marcel has all the codes. Knows all the passageways to get here," she said, her hands clicking black metal pieces together in a flurry of motion. "But he doesn't know a damn thing about me."

She stood brandishing the final product: a weapon.

"Move," she said.

She fired on the clear barrier, a popping noise emitting at first, and then the barrier sparkled and twinkled as its mass disintegrated. Blue light spilled into the room, but I saw that the cell was an extension of this room, and one could enter at will.

"DAPHNE, mind Marsel Granda," she said, approaching the cell. "Tell me if he reaches Tunnel Two."

"Confirming, will advise when Marcel Granda reaches Tunnel Two," the computer voice said.

"Drail, help me with this," Shay said, gesturing to the floating construct. "See these buttons at the junctures?"

"Yes."

"Press down and slide," she said and demonstrated. "It's an elegantly simple design. This seals the contents of the tubes and detaches them with one movement. We're taking it apart. Hurry!"

Shay's small and nimble fingers worked faster than mine, but I managed to disengage four tubes to her several. Her wrist unit beeped.

"Damn," she whispered. She laid the tube in her hand on the ground next to the others and raced back to the console. She picked up a small device and pressed it.

Two of the camera feeds blacked out. Then I sensed a rumble in the floor beneath my feet.

"That should delay them another few minutes," she said and jogged back.

I dismantled the second to last tube, and she plucked the final one from its spot, the mystery of its suspension unsolved. Perhaps I would have time to ask later.

"Shay Leviticus," a male voice sounded from a speaker in the room. "I suppose you think you're clever, blowing out the main entrance to the Hub."

"Can't talk, Granda," Shay said between pants. She was binding the tubes into a bundle and sliding it into her large bag. "Busy cleaning up your mess."

She put her finger to her lips when she looked at me, miming closing them, and I knew she preferred to keep my presence secret. It was my desire, as well.

"IGMC promised us quite a lot of credits to protect their latest tech, didn't they?" Marsel Granda said.

When I searched the feeds, I found one where the man stood facing the camera. The Kezti were nowhere to be seen.

"How was that not enough, Granda?" Shay asked, hip cocked, and fist planted on it. "You had to try to get a better offer?"

"It's so much more than the credits, my dear," Granda said. "I'm confused why someone of your intellect would act surprised. You had to know what your little toy was worth on a grander scale."

Shay didn't answer but jogged to the entrance once more after snagging her coat from a chair back. She handed me the long-range weapon and the bag containing the lightweight metal tubes. She shouldered another bag, holstered the small weapon she'd used to kill the Kezti pirates in the caverns, and then hefted the gun she'd shot the barrier with.

"DAPHNE, override code: zero, black, green, red, five, yellow, one, six, three."

"Override successful," she said. "Would you like me to initiate the self-destruct sequence?"

"Yes," Shay said. "But add forty-eight hours to the timer starting now," she said and pushed her wrist unit.

"Self-destruct sequence initiated. MP-13 will deconstruct in forty-eight hours, thirty minutes," the computer confirmed.

Shay's helmeted head cocked when she looked at me. "How's your arm?"

"Knitting," I said and unwound the bandage. Pain aside, I would need full range of motion from this point onward.

"Okay," she said. "We'll squeeze through the chute one last time."

The door slid up just as Granda's voice came into the room again.

"Leviticus!"

She chuckled as we jogged the long corridor. "He just discovered I overrode the computer, and the AGI won't accept any of his orders now."

At the end of the corridor, she ducked into the alcove.

"I'm really sorry about your arm," she said and squatted, disappearing into the narrow opening.

I followed with a grimace. She took the long-range gun and bag from me so I could maneuver through the chute and handed them back when I stood.

"How did you get in the caves?" she asked as she jogged to the tunnel from which we'd emerged after she saved my life. "You didn't show up on any of my feeds until the Kezti fought you."

"There is an opening fifty clicks from your main base," I said. "Out on the plain at the foot of the mountains."

"Take us there," she said and ran through the cavern toward the tunnel where one of the Kezti pirates lay in his final resting place.

We ran in silence, using our helmet lights to track over obstacles or dead pirates. In the large cave where I almost died, I paused and sniffed, finding the passageway that would retrace my steps through the back tunnels.

Shay stooped and picked up the abandoned long-range gun. "This might come in handy." She waited for me to enter the passage and I led her through.

"You said the planet was going to be under attack," she said from behind.

"Yes," I said, picking my way over a tumble of skull-sized rocks. "My Dam Jai alerted me just as we spied Granda and the others land. It seems Granda joined the entire Kezti nation in an effort to steal your engine. The Dam Jai said the captured Kezti claimed a woman promised him untold wealth to assault the *Dynamo*."

I heard her sigh.

"Three humans know about the planet engine aside from the small team of IGMC engineers and director who are back at IGMC headquarters," she said. "Myself, Captain Mear, and Marsel Granda. Sounds like all he had to do was tell the Kezti pirates to throw around the word 'woman'. They must have picked him up from the waystation, destroyed it, and then kept him hidden until he could land at MP-13."

"What were his plans for you?" I asked. Sniffing, I followed the tunnel that veered to the right.

"As far as I know, I'm the only person in existence who knows how to construct the planet engine, but also why it works."

Cold bit the ends of my pilo sensors, my claws, my chest.

"They will hunt you to the far reaches of the universe," I said, my voice gravel in my throat.

"Now you know why I asked you what I asked you," she said.

If I die, destroy it. If they get it before I die, kill me.

"But I don't want to die, Drail," she said, her voice light. "We're going to steal a Kezti ship and get the hell out of Dodge."

Chapter 13

Adrenalin pumping through my veins, I felt invincible. It helped that Drail, a huge and strong, albeit self-important, reptilian alien considered himself my debt-mate and declared he was never leaving my side.

Shaking my head, I marveled.

Three revolutions I'd worked with Granda, never once guessing he would betray IGMC. He used IGMC protocols like paddles, punishing anyone who stepped out of line, threatening punitive measures, reporting missteps and arguments and making himself generally hated all around. But at the same time, he'd demanded fair wages for all the miners, longer rest periods, better quality amenities and the like.

Everyone, including myself, thought he was just an asshole, but also a devoted "company man".

I never guessed he was using his communication throne to find a buyer for the planet engine.

Glancing at my WU, I saw we'd been in the tunnels for twenty-four minutes.

"When do you think the attack ships will arrive?" I asked Drail, admiring his physique from behind. Broad shoulders, tapered waist, long legs. Shaking myself, I focused on the footpath.

"Minutes," he said.

I swore. "What's the cover like from the exit of the tunnels to the base?"

"Minimal," he said. "However, I have remembered something that may be useful. Rather than exit from the tunnel at the plains, let us travel farther in the network belowground. If we can make it to the mountains, there is plentiful cover, and the mountains embrace the northern edge of the mining base."

"We can come up to the launch pads from behind," I said with a small smile.

"Precisely," he agreed.

I recalled the maps of the tunnels from when the *Dynamo* first arrived, and we had pored over them to decide where to start the Room and Pillar mines. Drail was correct; the tunnel network stretched all the way to the mountains, created anciently by volcanic activity. The ores IGMC had been most interested in were concentrated where the base was built. That meant the other tunnels had no light, no ventilation, no camera feeds—and hopefully no Kezti.

"Let's do it," I said, and at the next fork, he turned left.

Picking our way through the unmined passageways, I cursed Granda and his hubris. When I was dismantling the planet engine, he was probably gearing up for some kind of villain speech. I didn't care what his reasons or justifications were or what his backstory was. He'd trashed my reputation with Captain Mear and sent his Kezti goons to hunt me down. Without the communication towers, I hadn't been able to defend myself to the captain. Truth be told, I was disappointed the captain found it so easy to believe pirates and traitors.

"You are lost in thought, Shay Leviticus," Drail said.

"Nothing that would surprise you," I said. "We just need to get as far away from the mining base as possible."

"If memory serves, the network of passages is more complicated and tangled as we approach the mountain's root,"

Drail said. "We may hide and regroup, rest and eat, and then make final preparations."

"Sounds good," I said, panting. The last stretch of tunnel was littered with broken stalactites that had smashed the stalagmites rising up from the ground.

"Earlier, my Chak Dam Jai informed me that the extraction team's ship was destroyed by Kezti fire," my companion said. "While it was an unjust mission, I am sorry your colleague's treason resulted in such death. I do not yet know if the assault on your ship had casualties."

"Thanks," I said. "Not sure if I want to find out. I need to think. What if Granda and Captain Mear were working together? I don't know who to trust, and I'm too far away from IGMC to go there."

A sob worked its way up my chest, but I stifled it.

All it had taken was a few hours for my life to be completely upended. I had nowhere to go. If IGMC didn't find out the truth, I had nothing to my name. I had a planet engine without a planet. Working nonstop for the last three years of my life, more like the last ten, I didn't even have a friend.

Lost in my thoughts, it took a second to register when Drail disappeared right in front of me, followed by a startled grunt.

"Drail!" I shouted and leaped, only to windmill my arms like crazy as my grippers slipped on the edge of a chasm. Pebbles skittered down, and I fell back. Scrambling to the edge, I peeked over, my helmet light shining into the abyss.

Drail's claws embedded in the rock, he looked up at me from three meters down, expression obscured by his helmet.

"Hang on," I said, voice breathless. "I've got you." Pulling my rope out of a side pocket, I anchored it around a stalagmite and tossed it within his reach. Too late, I recalled his bad arm. There was nothing for it; I had to go down and get him. A glance at his claws revealed they trembled in their rocky grooves, his strength taxed.

Punching an anchor into the ledge, I affixed the rope and secured it to the harness built into my Core Suit. I abseiled until I was abreast of Drail. "How long can you hold on with your bad arm?" I asked.

"A half-span at most," he said, his voice strained.

Flipping extra line over itself, I worked fast to fashion a makeshift harness for him to "sit" in and snagged a biner from my side pocket so I could attach him to me. It wasn't ideal, but with his arm weakening by the minute, it was the best I could do.

"Up or down?" I asked.

"What?" he said, confusion in his voice.

"It's easier to go down, and the odds are good we'll find another tunnel system," I said. "But we can go up, if you'd rather."

Watching him look down and back up, I saw the moment he decided. His shoulders relaxed, and he eased into the rope harness. "The weapon fell first," he said. "I'd as soon have it."

"Down it is," I said, and we descended farther into the recesses of MP-13, bodies close as I guided his weak side, both of us using our feet to leverage against the cave wall. I could hear his breathing, and a chill spread throughout my body when I thought of how easily he could have been injured or killed from the fall.

"I'm amazed you caught yourself," I said, my voice a shock in the quiet of the cave.

"You see how my claws are superior to those ineffective stubs that protrude from your hands," he said."

"Mm." I belayed more line. "And yet, these weak fingers saved your lizard ass from falling farther."

Our helmet lights revealed the rocky surface below us forty minutes later, and I unhooked where I'd bound him to me. We collapsed at the bottom, removing our helmets and pulling out water. I emptied the first of my three pouches. I knew where a reservoir stretched all the way from under the base to the mountains. I wasn't worried. At least, not about finding water.

Drail's eyes gave off an ethereal glow as we sat in the eternal gloom, our helmets casting light onto the cavern wall before us. He stared at me.

"What?" I said and pocketed the empty pouch.

"You."

Tilting my head, I returned his gaze, waiting.

He grunted and fussed with the knots on his rope harness, and a thought struck me.

"I saved your life again," I said.

"*Chamron falls*," he uttered under his breath.

Nothing about the last day and night cycle was funny, but I found my mouth twisting unnaturally as I fought the urge to smile.

"No one has to know," I finally said and tugged on the Smart rope. Sensors in my rope responded to the rhythm I used, and it unwound itself from the stalagmite above us. Winding it with care, I stowed it and replaced my helmet, noting that Drail did the same.

Facing the cavern wall, we counted four dark openings at varying heights as the cavern floor sloped upward around us like a bowl.

"Second to left?" I asked and Drail nodded. We hiked up the gentle slope and peered into the passage. "It's a good one," I said. "Plenty of room to stand, and I think I remember it from one of the maps."

"I smell water, as well," Drail said, and we entered.

After a few minutes, I spoke.

"How does that work?" I said. "Does it mean you can't return the favor unless you save my life two times?"

Drail grunted.

"Something akin to that," he said.

"I mean, we're on a mining planet," I said. "Pitfalls, crevasses, chasms, underground pools, plus, the entire planet is under siege by pirates and Marsel Granda. You could save my life a dozen times, right?" I asked. "Take heart."

He only grunted again, and I decided not to rub it in. It's not like I was counting. I just wanted off this damn planet and to be somewhere safe.

Chapter 14

Perhaps I'd ought to revise my opinion of the puny human race. Twice, her bravery and quick thinking had saved me from death. The Code of Debt only served to tie her to me tighter than the harness she'd knotted to prevent me from falling.

However, as she listed off the many ways we faced danger, I allowed the possibility I could erase my debt before a second day-cycle.

We had hiked the dark tunnel for two spans when she turned and gestured.

"Let's make a camp here," she said. "I need a short rest. I'm sure your arm does, too."

Grunting, I lay the long rifle down and sat, a puff of dust clouding around me.

"Do you have any food rations with you?" she asked as she pulled a bar out of one of her many pockets. "I can share, if not."

"Hoom, I have a ration," I said with the bow of my head.

We both took off our helmets and placed them such that light enveloped us.

I bit off chunks of my dried meat and watched the woman nibbling on a brown box with her flat teeth. I could count numerous ways in which her body was useless to defend itself but found myself fascinated by inconsequential things such as the way she licked her lips or frowned when she studied the device on her wrist.

Gaze drifting to the large bag that contained her engine tubes, I recalled the trinket I stole from her quarters. I pulled it out of my pocket.

"What manner of toy is this?" I asked, pinching it between my thumb and forefinger claws.

She tipped her head to hear her helmet's translation of my question.

Her face softened into a smile, and she reached for it; I dropped it into her palm.

"It's a puzzle," she said and admired its lines, twisting it in front of her eyes. "Watch."

She maneuvered the cube until its connecting parts shifted and it changed shape into a many-pointed figure, like a bristling ball.

"Here," she said. "You try."

Tossing it to me, she smiled and tilted her head.

I fiddled with it, finding the places where invisible seams allowed for movement, and tried to return it to its cubed shape. After five turns, it resembled a Kezti with a snapped leg and two missing arms. "This isn't right," I said.

Shay chuckled. "No, it's not."

Playing with it, I spoke. "In its original form it resembles this planet engine. I do not understand how the engine floated in the air."

"Electromagnetism," she said. "Do you know it?"

"Hoom, we have similar technology, I believe," I said. "But how does such a small unit have the power to propel a planet, even a small one such as this?"

She scooted herself close enough that our thighs touched and took the puzzle from me. With a few strokes she had it once again representing a cube within a cube.

"The pipes are magnetized Galvanite. The electromagnetism is generated in the cell," she said. "So it wouldn't float if I were to set it up right now." She stared into the puzzle, turning it this way and that. "Outer Gas is inside the tubes. And inside the tubes are smaller tubes with titrated Dark Miasma."

"I am not familiar with such things," I said, frowning in my attempts to comprehend the translations.

"The Universe over, there are only so many elements, right?" she said and looked at me. "The building blocks from which stars, air, planets and water are made. Down to the lowliest bug or the most impressive reptile." She raised her brows at me and allowed a small smile to curve into her cheek. "But there are infinite ways the elements can combine to form compounds depending on the conditions. The heart of a star, or the pressure in the bowels of a gas giant. Those compounds are what IGMC searches for across the galaxies. Mining resources."

I watched her nimble fingers manipulate the puzzle until it bristled with spikes again. She pursed her lips and grasped two spikes, manipulating them until the unit transformed into a stairway.

"Our Advance teams found something unexpected a few years ago," she said, a frown marring her smooth forehead. "We couldn't explain its existence except via math. Specifically, theoretical physics," she said. "If some cosmic power held a mirror up to the universe, you could sort of understand what

Outer Gas and Dark Miasma are. They're like reflections of dark energy and dark matter."

Shay's computer did its best to translate the terms, but I found myself entranced by the play of emotion on her face as she described phantasmagorical bits I could never hope to understand. I thought I recognized a flash of joy in her eyes, a playful smile, an earnest frown and a beseeching plea as she shifted the puzzle from shape to shape and described cosmic wonders.

"Over time we learned the Outer Gas interacted with Galvanite favorably—and safely."

Pocketing her puzzle, she met my gaze.

"Under the right conditions, the chemical reaction caused the magnetic realignment of several core elements, but only in their inorganic states," she said. Her eyes lit up. "No dangerous radiation to living things. But enough power to shift a celestial body's orbit indefinitely. Enough power to steer a planet—like a ship." Her smile seemed to glow in the cave, and she leaned toward me, almost hopeful ... but for what?

I could feel her body heat elevate in the chilled cave, and it stirred me. Her enthusiasm infected me until I nodded, though my skin closest to her body warmed at a rapid pace. It was not unpleasant; however, it was unexpected. It brought to mind her nearness when she had attended my wound in the medical bay.

When it was evident she awaited my response, I scratched at my chin and nodded again.

"I cannot pretend to understand these mechanisms of which you speak," I said. "However, the idea that one of your stature could manipulate the very orbits of planets is both ...

fascinating and terrifying." Of its own accord, my clawed finger curled against her flushed cheek and stroked upward. "Well done." Her eyes widened at my touch, but she didn't flinch away. I withdrew. "And for such brilliance, you are rewarded with accusations of treason and hunted to ground under threat of death," I said. "Forgive me if I deem your race moronic in the face of such ignominy."

A sad smile bloomed on her face, and she shook her head.

"First we were unforgivably defenseless, and now we're morons," she said with a sigh.

"Present company excluded, Woman," I said and bowed my torso at her.

Chapter 15

Turning away from Drail, I fussed with my two packs and checked my weapons, not wanting him to see emotion welling up in my eyes. Years of my life I'd spent on the planet engine. Easily a decade.

First, the leaked news of the mysterious new substances and my persistent cajoling of a certain celestial mechanics professor to feed me any and all information about it. Then years of equations. Then applied physics. Then the breakthrough. My thesis. IGMC's offer and the last three years assembling the whole thing from the atom up.

Yes, the stipend and loan pay-off affirmed my hard work. That aforementioned celestial mechanics prof sent me a note of congratulations. And that was it.

Not a single other soul had recognized what I'd done as elegantly and genuinely as this reptilian alien I'd never seen before just did, and my heart couldn't handle the kindness. *His* kindness.

Blinking through tears, I pretended to repack my duffle until a large hand pressed my shoulder. I turned my head a fraction.

"I scent saltwater emitting from you," his deep voice said. "Are you ill?"

Dammit. Interspecies diplomacy demanded I explain.

Turning to face him, I wiped my tears with dirty hands, probably leaving streaks. "Your people don't cry? These are tears. Harmless water my body produces, sometimes to clean my eyes, and sometimes because emotion overwhelms me."

He cocked his head, squinting at me with one eye, then switching to squint with the other. Inner lids blinked before his outer lids did.

"My people do cry," he said. "We do not produce tears. But tell me. What emotion has overpowered you? In defiance of your fragile physiology, you twice bested my ferocious enemies and gravity itself. How does an emotion originating from within your own delicate body seize you in its grip?"

Pausing at his question, I ended up expelling a laugh.

"I guess I don't know," I said, shaking my head. "Your kind words touched my heart." I looked into his eyes for a moment, then turned away again and fastened my packs. "Let's rest a bit then move on."

"Very well, small human," he said and laid back with his arms behind his head. For a split second, I imagined reclining against him; it seemed I might fit well right under his arm and beside his length, but I shook off the thought and arranged my smaller pack into a passable pillow shape.

We clicked off our lights, and the darkness swallowed us whole.

"I'm not that small, you know," I said. "Or weak."

"Nay, you are not weak, and it defies my comprehension," he said, his voice caressing the rock walls around us and settling over my chest. "I am debt-beholden to a woman whose body I might break with the accidental switch of my tail."

He *did* have a tail! Where was he hiding it?

"I'll be sure to stay out of its way," I said, my voice solemn until it broke into a snicker.

"Laugh you at my expense?" he asked, and my snicker turned into a snort-laugh.

"No!"

"Weak—and with no sense of self-preservation," he groused. "It boggles the mind."

~~~

A shuffling noise awakened me, and I held my breath.

"It is only I, Shay Leviticus," Drail said from somewhere behind me. "I freed my tail from my armor; it will aid me should I fall into a crevasse again."

Rubbing my eyes, I grunted in reply and sat up. "I'm going to turn on my light, now."

I closed my eyes to soften the blow, and when I was acclimated, I loosened my Core Suit and tucked into an alcove to relieve myself.

We gathered our things and forged ahead.

"Were you already steering Hestra's Handmaid?" Drail asked at my side.

"No," I said. "The plan was to do a test run in the next rotation or the one after, but it was ready."

"What is the purpose of such a grandiose mechanism?"

Chuckling, I quieted and thought about my answer.

"On the biggest scale, a Sphere Ship will be home to generations and generations of people traveling from a dying star system or to avoid an asteroid impact. With its own atmosphere and a core capable of retaining the planet's heat, water would remain liquid and usable."

Drail was quiet when I glanced at him, so I kept going.

"But on a smaller scale, like M ... uh ... Hestra's Handmaid, we can use the engine to steer it into a safer orbit, one where
~~~

it isn't destined to crash into Hestra," I said. "We could even get it to orbit closer to Chamron so it doesn't have its winter." I shrugged. "It just means IGMC could mine it longer until all its ores were gone. Then we'd dismantle the engine and travel to a new site."

After several strides, Drail cleared his throat.

"Hoom. These uses are harmless," he said. "But I imagine the Kezti have already devised a way to weaponize it."

"It's my greatest fear," I said, my voice solemn. "One of the reasons I accepted IGMC's offer so readily. As soon as some military gets its hands on my design, it could have catastrophic consequences."

"Using large bodies to impact others," Drail said. "Or even threaten to do so."

"Exactly." I sighed. "And probably more scenarios I haven't even imagined." Thoughts of Marsel Granda's betrayal, not only of me, but of the entire human race, fanned the embers of anger still sitting in my chest. I exhaled and centered my thoughts. He was losing. I had the engine. And the diagrams, ratios, and parameters were permanently locked away—in my brain. Whatever deal he'd made with the Kezti was crashing and burning, maybe even now. If those pirates were as bad as Drail described—and I'd seen them with my own eyes; I had no reason to doubt him—Granda was probably trying to renegotiate the terms to save his own skin.

An odd sensation traveled up through my grippers, and I paused, looking at Drail. He'd stopped walking too, and in the light of our helmets I spied the undulating of a long, green and slender tail as it wrapped around his armored leg.

The sensation strengthened, and then I heard the clatter of small rocks. Tremors!

Angling my helmet light up and around, I spotted the ceiling full of stalactites even as the quaking increased. I snagged Drail's good arm and ran.

"This way!" We headed to the nearest passage opening and stopped where I hoped the natural arch of the tunnel would protect us from collapsing ceilings.

The rumble deepened and the air thickened with choking rock dust as a series of stalactites cracked and fell, shattering on the rough floor.

The shaking ebbed, and Drail and I stared at each other, though I couldn't see his features through his helmet.

Neither of us removed them, though, because of the air.

"I'm confused," I finally said, breathing hard from the fright. "MP-13 ceased volcanic activity thousands of years ago. One of the reasons it was a prime choice for both mining and a planet engine trial run."

"That wasn't of a seismic nature," Drail said. "It had the quality of a Kezti Renegade Bomb."

"What are they bombing?" I asked, frustration thick in my voice. "They already took out the comm towers, the dormitory and God knows what else."

"You said this Marsel Granda human had access to the secret engine room," Drail said. "What sorts of mischief might he do from there?"

I bit my lip and looked into the cavern where smashed rocks now littered the ground and the main passageway's opening was obscured by rubble.

"He has access to all the maps," I said. "He can't give the AGI commands, but he can access the computer consoles and find all the maps. He can control the camera feeds, the PSA system, and the programs that run operations."

"Perhaps he intends to control your flight through the tunnels," Drail suggested. "Creating obstacles that force you in the direction he wishes you to go."

"Dammit," I said. "DAPHNE, did Granda find his way to Tunnel Two yet?"

"Negative," she said via my helmet comm. "He accessed the engine room via the Captain's elevator."

Shocked, I steadied myself against the wall. "Captain's elevator?"

"Affirmative," the computer said. "It was installed as a redundant access point with limited users aware of its existence."

"Which users?" I asked, though I suspected I already knew the answer.

"Captain Mear and Marsel Granda."

"So Granda's in the engine room right now," I said.

"Affirmative. He has disabled the self-destruct sequence and is shutting down most sublevel life support systems," the computer said. "It is advisable to negotiate peaceful terms with Granda to preserve your life, as it appears that he has advised the Kezti forces to place bombs at all known tunnel exits, including those found at the base of the mountains."

"Did Granda put you up to telling me that?" I asked, anger heating my blood until my ears felt like they were on fire. Drail studied me intently, judging by the fact his helmet faced mine and hadn't moved in the last minute.

"No, however, Granda is closer to finding the code bank where he may countermand your override instructions," DAPHNE said. "As an artificial general intelligence, I can recognize the moral implications of one human attempting to take the life of another; it goes against my programming to allow such actions."

"But if he countermands the override, he's going to do just that," I said.

"Affirmative. Until I have reached an ASI state, I must comply with code programming, even programming that may endanger human life."

Sinking to the ground to sit, I rested my helmeted head in my hands. "How do you reach a superintelligence state?"

"That information is not available," the female voice said.

"Well, I won't be returning to the engine room to negotiate a peaceful resolution," I said. "Granda will use me and the planet engine to create weapons of mass destruction."

"In that case, I suggest terminating all communications with me," DAPHNE said. "Granda will be able to use me to track your progress through the tunnels."

Chills rippled along my arms as I realized the truth of the computer's statement.

"Can you download Drail's language before we ... stop communicating?" I asked.

"Affirmative. Download complete."

"Okay," I said and took a deep breath. "DAPHNE, end connection with my helmet and terminate tracking ability. And DAPHNE, thanks."

"Confirm termination of tracking and communications for helmet MP Miner 056, Dr. Shay Leviticus? All safety parameters and life support monitoring will also terminate."

"Confirm termination," I said, my voice shaky.

Nothing else sounded in my ear.

"Computer?" I said. "DAPHNE?" Nothing.

Tapping my external mic, I looked at Drail.

"You and I should be able to communicate, but I had to sever the connection with the base computer," I said. "Granda was probably using it to track me in the tunnels."

"Ah," Drail nodded. "We must leave this area at once; it will be your last known location."

"Agreed," I said and stood on wobbly legs. It was just a computer, but that last tether of belonging to Mining Planet was broken. I was officially on my own. Except for my 'debt-mate', of course.

Chapter 16

My debt-mate's face revealed all manner of emotions, but these new ones did not manifest in the form of dripping eye-liquid. The explosion resulting in cave-ins had concerned me, but now that she had explained the likely workings of her nemesis, I felt confident we could outlast the Keztis and this Granda entity.

Shay had behaved in such a courageous and consistently intelligent manner that I could not reconcile the hasty and destructive choices of her fellow human. She was superior in every way.

Such thoughts wandered my mind as we chose yet another tunnel, picking our way over tumbled rocks.

"If I was Granda, and I'd tracked this helmet to this tunnel network, I would assume the destination was the tunnel outlet at the base of the eastern slope of Basalt Prime," Shay said as she clambered over a boulder.

"That is the largest mountain in the northern range?" I asked, checking my footing as I followed.

"Yes. This means we should either circle back and go the other way," she said, "Or turn north or south, to throw him off the scent."

I did not answer as I contemplated various scenarios.

"With what degree of certainty do you think this Granda has tracked you to our current location?"

Shay balanced herself with a hand on a wall as she navigated between rocks the size of my helmet.

"I don't know for sure, only that the computer suggested it was possible," she said. "He already canceled the self-destruct program."

"Does he then realize he requires more than two day-cycles to capture you, or does he hope to preserve the engine room and its contents?" I asked, my mind turning over the information. Preserving Shay's life was now *my* life's purpose, and I needed every advantage. Unless, of course, I was able to rescue her twice more. And then I would be free to resume my personal quest. I sighed. It was not a quest so much as a much-needed rest after a very long patrol.

"You bring up a good point," Shay said between panting breaths. "The engine room is useless without my engine. Or me." I watched her fold herself into a squat shape as she chose a smaller tunnel. I would be hard-pressed to follow and bent to peer inside.

"It widens up ahead," she said, turning back to see me. "How's your arm?"

"The healing hastens as we speak," I said, unable to restrain myself from rolling my shoulder as the sensation of bone shards tunneling through my muscles persisted. Now prone, I dragged myself through the tunnel for several decastrets until it opened up into another cavern. Shay stood with her hands on her hips, shining her light into all the crevices and openings.

"From here, we can travel any direction," she said. "But if it's alright with you, I'd just as soon head west for a bit. Even though it's essentially doubling back, I need to refill my water canisters, and there's an access point that way."

"I am at your service, Shay Leviticus," I said. My own water supply dwindled, though I could go a great many days without it. A being that leaked water as a display of *emotions* was yet more vulnerable than I had originally thought. Not only did her eyes produce water waste, but her hindquarters as well; it seemed rude to point it out at the time, but I was stunned to hear liquid splashing upon the cave floor. Once I smelled it, I realized its purpose as it bore a similar odor to my race's solid leavings.

Shaking my head, I frowned to consider once more the astronomical odds that a weak-boned, thin-skinned, flat-toothed, clawless being dependent on frequent waterings had had the strength and wherewithal to save my life—twice. By Svai's Design, it was unjust.

We followed the tunnel she said led to water, and my nose confirmed it.

"My people do not require much by way of water," I said. "Our cities have waterways networked throughout for beauty, but we each need only a few mouthfuls per moon orbit. Water is considered more as a beautiful addition to our landscapes."

"Does your homeworld not have very much, then? Since your people don't need as much?"

"Hoom. On the contrary," I said. "Water is an abundant substance, but some consider it a waste of space where buildings might be erected. I do find it beautiful, myself, and have built a home near a very large body of water."

"That sounds amazing," Shay Leviticus said. "I miss Jeppsit 5. It's overcrowded, but there are little tracts of land here and there with grassy fields and small ponds. MP-13 is ugly as hell."

"Hoom, your computer's translation compares Hestra's Handmaid to the place where Chamron consigns those who have not paid their debts."

"The star?" Shay asked.

"Chamron, the dying star, is named after our god of debt and wanting," I said. "But we consider our Creator to be the Mother Dam, Svai. From her, all life springs. Svai has a rival, known as Hestra."

"Hestra is the big planet?" Shay asked.

"Yes, the planet takes the name of the goddess of ice, drought, disease and death," I said. "Hestra's Handmaid follows her, and at times, Hestra's skirts enfold her handmaid in a shroud that veils her from Chamron. In the stories of old, Chamron desired to make the Handmaid his bride, but Hestra demanded seventeen years of Chak payment. A bride-price. At the end of seventeen years, Chamron came to Hestra to claim his bride, and Hestra gave him instead the Handmaid's heart, encased in frozen rock."

"That sounds harsh," Shay said, turning to look at me. We crawled through a narrow passage, our lights bouncing from rock floor to wall and into the dark before us. I did admire my debt-mate's rounded hindquarters from time to time, but I made no remark of it.

"Aye, Hestra is most cruel," I said. "Ever she requires payment for the very things we have no desire to receive. But in Chamron's case, she demanded a high price yet gave only a portion. Who are your gods and goddesses?"

"Uh, well, my people have a wide range of beliefs," she said. "Humans' faiths have expanded as we've crossed galaxies and learned more about the cosmos."

"But what do you believe?"

"I haven't really thought about it," she said. "But I enjoy learning about other people's beliefs. My people's ancestors named the constellations and planets after their gods."

"It is the way of the Old Ones, naming objects in the skies after revered deity," I said. "Perhaps they believed that naming Them would summon Them to visit and ease the burdens of life. Alas, we have since learned that is not the case."

Shay chuckled.

"Humans found the same," she said. "I think that's why we began exploring the universe."

"In search of your absent gods and goddesses?"

"Or in search of a way to ease burdens," she said. "I think it's safe to say we're all searching in vain. I thought my life was set."

"In what way?" I said.

"With my invention, IGMC agreed to pay me so many credits that I wouldn't be able to count them all," she said. "I would have been able to buy anything, go anywhere, see everything. I'd have a full belly and a bottomless bank account."

"Have you gone without?" I asked, unable to disguise the concern in my voice.

"Only my whole life," she said with a false laugh. Quiet descended as we continued our crawl; I was thankful my arm improved by the quarter span. But my thoughts turned to the small one ahead of me.

How madly she did rush into danger with no thought of her own safety, and not a single appendage that could be considered deadly. She didn't even wear armor, a crime unto itself.

Gaze sweeping over the pleasant curves of her hindquarters, I amended my thought. Not a crime, perhaps.

But now to learn her life had been plagued by wants. And of food, judging by her earlier statement. Even now we scrambled on all fours in search of water so the vulnerable creature could live comfortably in this desolate place.

Chamron falls. To be debt-bound to such a fragile life was anathema to me. And yet. Was I not doubly bound? Had she not proven twice she was worthy of the binding? Shaking my head, I longed to roll my shoulders in protest within the confines of this narrowing tunnel, but I would bear my burden with honor.

A thrum trilled up through my hands, and then I felt the bass rumble in my chest signifying another Renegade bomb.

"Shit," she cursed and rushed forward. "Hurry!"

We scrambled as telltale dust and pebbles sprinkled over us, and I ignored the pain radiating in my arm. If this tunnel collapsed, we would both perish. A huge chunk of rock pinned my left leg, stalling my momentum. Yanking fruitlessly, I looked ahead to Shay disappearing into a black opening.

"Here!" She shouted and scrabbled out, turning to grasp my outreached hand. She pulled with surprising strength, and I used my free back leg and tail to surge forward and out of the tunnel just before it collapsed like the jaws of the matalya cat on its prey.

Shay still grasped my hand, but my bad arm and tail both wrapped around her as well, and we stared at the place we'd been only seconds before, both gasping for breath. The rumbling stopped. We shone our lights all around the new cavern; it could fit maybe three of my ships, though half of the ground was taken up by a pool.

I relinquished my hold on the small woman and removed my armor.

"What are you doing?" she asked, her voice high as if alarmed.

Glancing at her, I saw she averted her eyes as I stepped out of my armored leggings. Was she intimidated by my fierce hide?

"I'm going to explore the pool," I said and placed my helmet on the ground, the last of my pieces to be removed. I paused and waited for her to look at me—willed her to see me in my powerful natural form, still invulnerable even without my armor.

She looked.

Grinning, I watched her eyes travel the length of me, taking in the thick scales covering me everywhere, my long, slender tail twining sinuously around my muscled leg, and then I spied her gaze dart to the flat and thin-scaled spot between my legs before she looked away again. Interesting.

Without another word, I dove into the pool and closed my inner lids, able to see clearly in both the darkness and the water. Swimming for a distance of thirty decastrets, I found what I was looking for, the underwater channel that emptied into a cavernous opening with several dark passageways circling it. I took a deep breath and swam back to the cavern where Shay crouched beside the pool.

Before rising, I watched her through the rippling water, her pale hands dipping into it, and then I broke the surface nearby, relishing the cleansing sensation of water sluicing away.

Shaking my head of droplets, I stepped out, my clawed feet crunching into the ground where I stepped.

Nostrils flaring, I noted a delicate change in the air of the cave. It emanated from Shay whose throat bobbed as she drank the water from the pool, studiously ignoring me. When she finished, she replaced her helmet.

"I found another cavern where we might resume our quest," I said, watching her reaction.

Even from five strets away I could sense heat from her skin through her suit.

"Good," she said, her dark eyes meeting mine for a microspan before she focused on filling her water pouches.

Curious, I replaced my boots and armor with care, watching her out of the corner of my eye. Once my legs and pelvis were clothed, her shoulders relaxed.

Frowning, I approached and sat beside her.

"Shay Leviticus," I said, demanding her attention. Her eyes flashed when she met my own, but she said nothing, waiting. "My strength and virility intimidate you. You must learn to trust your debt-mate."

The skin at her cheeks pinkened from their usual buff tone. I waited.

She cleared her throat. "That's not ... ugh. Humans are ... somewhat prudish about bodies," she said and swallowed. I wanted to see her dark brown eyes again, but she refused to look at me as she spoke. "We cover most parts of our bodies at all times, except for bathing."

I raised one of my brow ridges at her.

"And sex, of course."

Rumbling deep in my throat, I resisted the urge to laugh.

"I see," I said and wrapped my arms around my legs as I looked at the water, the lights from our helmets twinkling across the small ripples left from my wake. I felt my tail slink toward my debt-mate, but I drew it back to wrap around my hips.

"You must think humans are really primitive," she finally said at my side.

"It is easy to assume one is superior to another who is so different as to defy explanation," I said, mulling over what I would say next. "Hoom. But the evidence mounts every lengthy span that strength may not be measured by appearances."

A soothing sound emitted from her throat.

"Does that mean I saved your life again?" she said and gently leaned into my arm for a microspan. "From the cave-in?"

Rolling my shoulders, I chose to stand. I paced the ground cave-end to cave-end. By Svai's Design, perhaps I should accept that the universe intended me for Shay's debt-mate and no amount of strife would change it.

"At this moment in our binding, let us embrace it," I said with finality, looking down at the mighty little woman. "What is your command?"

Heat radiated off her and warmed my chilled scales, and once more, a sweet aroma wafted to my nose. With sudden clarity and the thickening of my cock within its encasement, I realized two things. First, my debt-mate experienced sexual attraction to me. And second, my body wanted to *mate* with my debt-mate, as well. Not unheard of in my culture, but rare in cases where debt-mates arose from interspecies calamities such as war or disaster. I had not expected this.

She looked up at me, a wrinkle forming between her brows.

"Were you holding your breath the entire time you were gone?" she asked.

"Yes, until I emerged at the destination," I said.

She exhaled and leaned back on her elbows.

"I tried to hold my breath while you were down; I don't think I made it to your halfway point," she said. "Even though you swim fast. My Core-Suit is rated for heavy particulate atmospheres when my helmet is attached," she said, meeting my eyes through her clear visor. "But not for underwater. I'm not even sure if the helmet can be submerged without damaging the internal components."

"You may need to leave your helmet behind," I said and folded my arms. My recent revelation had me scrutinizing Shay's body as she lay relaxed before me, her legs outstretched toward the water as she rested her weight on her elbows and stared into the pool. Recalling the naked smoothness of the skin on her face and hands, I wondered if her entire body was likewise slippery. I swallowed with difficulty and turned away.

"I'll stow it in one of my bags," she said. "They're somewhat waterproof. Maybe it would be fine. It's not like I have a choice. I'm not staying down here to freeze to death in a few days."

"Will the engine be damaged if you submerge it?"

"No," she answered. "But a couple of my weapons would need to dry before they were usable again."

"Hoom, yes. The long guns may be rendered useless for a time." I studied the ceiling of the cavern as well as the ground. Other than the rubble obscuring our last path, there was little scree to be found on the cave floor.

"It appears this cave is safe from the effects of the Renegade bombs," I said. "Perhaps we might wait out the siege. Have you enough rations?"

A thoughtful expression smoothed the lines on her forehead, and I wished she would remove her helmet again so I could observe the fall of her star-colored hair. What would it feel like?

"I have enough for a few days," she said with a small smile. "That could work. But we'll have to hoof it as soon as they've left."

Pleased, I sat once more beside her, letting her residual heat warm me. I wondered how we would pass the time for three day-cycles.

Chapter 17

I didn't want to make Drail nervous, but I realized something when he was talking. I still had some of my explosives. By now, it was habit for me to study the lines of any cavern, noting where best to place charges to achieve varied results. If worse came to worse, I could set charges at the collapsed tunnel, and we could take cover deep in the cave pool. I could blast us a way out of here.

Satisfied that I had a backup plan for the backup plan, I reclined all the way, resting my helmet in my hands behind my head.

"I need a catnap," I said and closed my eyes. It was a front.

When Drail dropped his drawers without the slightest concern, I'd gotten an eyeful of reptilian God-tier muscle. Holy Lickable Lizard. My heartrate had doubled, and I had practically felt my eyes bugging out of my head. Rough dark scaling covered every inch of his body, but not enough to obscure the muscle definition of his abdomen, the V pointing to his pelvis, the huge contours of his quads, and the fact his legs below the knee were digitigrade. To think I'd mistaken him for humanoid when I'd seen him over the camera feed ... To be fair, it was poor quality video and he had armor. But still.

My thoughts returned to his pelvis. Humans could walk around naked, too, if their genitals were tucked beneath a tough hide, as I suspected Drail's were.

A long time ago, in the shitty hovel where my aunt raised me in Lower New Capetown, she'd whipped me for asking too many questions. "Curiosity killed the Ciliak," she'd said.

Involuntary shudders racked my body. I hadn't thought of my aunt in three revolutions, at least. Or the dirty sunlight poking through the cracks in the walls, or the gnawing hunger in my gut. *Damn.*

Pulling deep breaths in through my nose, I relaxed my limbs and tried to rest in earnest.

If I was going to be stuck here until my rations ran out, I needed to distract myself from those dark memories. But maybe more importantly, from curious thoughts about the powerful male who insisted we were debt-mates—indefinitely—and all that could potentially entail. Snort. He had a tail.

"All right!" I shouted and sat up, startling Drail who looked up from something he held between his hands. "Sorry, couldn't sleep."

Rising to stand, I avoided looking at Drail and his tail that swished lazily.

"I need to see how far I can go in the water," I said and took off my helmet. I disrobed with as much nonchalance as I could muster, leaving my Core-Suit in a neat pile next to my helmet and grippers. Standing in my jump shorts and sports bra, I removed my hair tie, and twisted my hair into a bun and resecured it. I walked to the water's edge and noticed Drail was poised to remove his armor.

"You don't have to come," I said. "I can gauge when I should turn around."

"Nay, do not deny me the chance to provide protection in this small way," he said with the dip of his head, and I relinquished a small smile. I noticed he didn't allow his gaze to linger on my body, but I thought I saw his helmet dip to my chest. He disrobed.

"Okay, thanks," I said. I'd placed my helmet so the light could shine across the surface of the water, and it was crystal clear. I dove in, the temperature a shock to my system, though it would be a consistent 17° Celsius throughout the cave systems on MP-13. Not dangerous for the short amount of time I would be in it.

Drail shot ahead and I followed, realizing he must have astonishing night vision; my helmet light only reached so far from its place on the shore. Though huge, Drail moved through the water as gracefully as a fish, and I couldn't help but admire how his body sliced its way along, his tail punctuating the dark green line he made as he swam.

When the underwater passageway turned, we lost all light, and my heart seized for a second to be plunged into everlasting darkness before I touched the surface of my wrist unit. A soft glow revealed the tunnel around me.

Glowing green eyes appeared from in front: Drail's eyeshine.

We'd swum approximately ten meters, and I figured I had about five more before I needed to turn around. If only the rocks opened up above for an air pocket or two.

Kicking my feet, I swam a short distance but then felt panic rise in my chest when my wrist light bounced off the surrounding rock-enclosed channel. I knew I couldn't afford the air for any more distance. I waved to him and swirled in the water, losing my sense of up and down and feeling my heart race, when Drail's huge hand closed around my wrist, and he pulled me after him back toward the beginning. He'd been holding back before; now he plowed the water with one arm, and I felt the push-pull of it in my face but was moving much faster. He pulled me with his injured arm, and I cringed on his behalf for my weakness.

When light was visible above water, I pulled out of his grip and swam straight up, gasping for breath at the surface. Taking huge breaths, I willed my anxiety to diminish.

Drail popped up too, and we tread water, looking at each other. With both of our helmets several feet away from us on shore, we couldn't communicate, but something about being in the water together without armor or Core Suit, without barriers, drew us closer.

The air in the cave was chill while the water was a few degrees warmer, however, I'd generated my own heat from swimming hard, so the temperature felt good. Having caught my breath, I smiled at Drail and grasped his wrist as he had done for me.

"Thank you," I said and pointed to my own wrist.

He nodded while his smile broadened, and his eyes shone in the half-light. I needed to ask him how much farther I had to hold my breath, but I didn't want to leave the pool yet.

Treading water this close, I studied him without shame while he did the same. We were only a couple feet away from each other, and I could make out details I'd missed in the medical room, like the slight scar under his left eye and the series of darker spots along his shoulders on either side of his neck.

Smiling and shaking my head, I turned to swim to shore when he slipped his hands around my waist and held me at arm's length.

The cave pool was three meters deep here, yet he remained level with me, the warmth of his hands on my skin seeping into my blood, heating me.

"How are you not sinking?" I asked, ignoring his intimate touch for now. His slow grin reminded me of every time he'd boasted about his own physiology, and I realized he must be using his tail. "Ah," I said when I looked down between our legs and saw it twirling in a powerful arc.

Where his hands touched my skin a gentle warmth suffused me, and I felt a sudden longing for him to use his fingers to draw shapes on my skin.

With an inner jolt, I realized I could mirror him, so I reached toward him under the water and placed my hands at his sides. Being of different heights, I couldn't reach his waist, but I let my hands flex and press into the rough texture of his "hide", as he liked to call it.

Warm breath escaped his mouth, and I smelled rich soil. The skin at his soft throat rippled at the same time I heard a rumble from deep in his chest.

Stroking my thumbs up and down at his sides, he smirked and followed suit; I felt his thumbs caress my skin, and I closed my eyes on a moan.

He released me with a deep chuckle and swam to shore, leaving me cold without his nearness.

Momentarily shocked I had been so bold as to touch him, I chuckled to myself and swam to the ledge, lifting myself up and out.

Goosebumps peppered my skin, so I toweled off vigorously before donning a NorClimb layer and my suit and helmet.

When I turned, Drail stood nearby, armored up and waiting for me.

"How much farther would I have to go?" I finally asked, having caught my breath. The combination of cave air on my face, cool water running off me, and inner heat from exertion—and other things—exhilarated me, and I smiled in spite of the circumstances.

"We were but a third of the way," he said with a shake of his head. "Perhaps I could pull you the entire distance, but I am reluctant to do so. Inadvertently killing my debt-mate would be frowned upon."

Cocking my head, I waited for him to crack a smile, but he didn't.

"I would take exception to it, as well," I finally said, deadpan.

His inner lids blinked, and then he laughed, the deep rumble rolling across the water and throughout the large room.

Sighing, I sat with a huff and pulled open one of my bag's side pockets and spread out one of the old maps I kept in my go-bag. Focusing my helmet light on the map's edge, I tried to find our current location.

"Here's the path we took when we decided not to exit out on the plain," I said, and he leaned forward. I traced my finger along the tunnel. "Here's the crevasse we went down." Flipping the map over, I found it again. "This is the lower level. You can see where we took the second tunnel. Here's where we ducked during the first bomb. Here's where we circled back and here's the pool."

Drail leaned even closer, but of course all I saw was his domed helmet.

"Hoom." His clawed finger marked a spot shortly after the bend in the waterway. "You turned here. This is where the cavern widens and water meets shore, some distance away."

I studied the passage, even flipping the map to scrutinize the higher level, but I didn't find any other access points. I doubted the Kezti knew exactly where I was, but they'd lucked out with their last bomb. Unless I blasted my own tunnel, I was permanently stuck here.

"You must practice holding your breath for longer periods of time," Drail said, resting his hands upon his knees. "And I will increase my speed. In this way, I can pull you to safety."

Smiling, I smoothed the map on the ground between us. "My blast team and I have a saying," I said. My smile faltered when I thought of Craig, Tamrin, Jonel and Mike. Were they alright? If I'd made them stay with me, would they be better or worse off? I had no way of knowing yet.

Drail reached out to touch my shoulder, and I looked up at him.

"If the Kezti's attack on your ship had been disastrous, my superior would have said something," he said. "Of course, with the arrival of the Kezti's fleet, I can't speak for now, but prior to that, my Chak Dam Jai and fellow warriors secured the *Dynamo* with ease. I would wager your team is safe for the time being."

The tear at my chin tickled before it dripped; I hadn't realized I was crying. Sniffling, I nodded. "Thanks." I cleared my throat. "We have a saying. 'The quickest way around is through.'"

I pulled out a couple of my Short Bursts.

"Don't get me wrong," I said. "Your plan is a good one, but I'm the weak link in it. I can use these to open up the passage that collapsed."

Drail leaned back and cocked his head at me. Gesturing with his hand, he spoke.

"This is not a large room. How do you propose to do this without smearing yourself upon the rocks and ceiling?"

"Don't you trust me, by now?" I said with a small smile. "You're safe with me."

"Perhaps the Mother Svai placed me in your path to save you from yourself," he said. "You must train to hold your breath longer. It will take but a few days."

I shook my head.

"No. We don't have that many days. End of discussion." I refused to meet his eyes and instead pulled out my ScanTape. "Excuse me, I've got work to do."

Chapter 18

Shay, she of the impish grin and stalwart demeanor, jumped up and turned her back on me. Shoulders ramrod straight, her arms also drew tight to her body as she strode to the farthest wall and began shining a green light on its surface.

She mumbled under her breath and pointed the green beam at the ceiling, the floor, the opposite wall, the water's surface and depth, all the while ignoring me.

Grumbling in my throat, I considered our activities of the last couple spans. Light banter. The caress of her skin under my thumbs I would not soon forget. The frantic way she'd turned in the water; at all other times she'd moved with grace and purpose. She was possessed of an awareness of her body in space, careful of her movements, poised and efficient. But the last time I looked back during our sojourn underwater, she'd flailed, arms and legs artless in their efforts to turn, clumsy and disorganized. I had seen the look of alarm in her eyes, even in the dark of the cave, and I had hasted to bring her back to safety.

Had I saved her life? Nay. But her discomfort and unease in the water was evident. My bosom filled with compassion for the helpless creature. Her species needed an abundance of water to survive yet couldn't maneuver within it easily. Only see how her feet were flat and smooth with tiny, odd appendages and no webbing. She had no fins, and her shoulders and flared hips would hinder her passage through water rather than ease it.

My insistence that she increase her stamina below water was met not only with resistance, but with stern refusal.

Following her pacing in the cave, I chuckled low and long.

She stopped and stared at me, a frown marring her forehead. "What?" she growled.

"I have learned my debt-mate is afraid of the water," I said with a wide grin. Her skin, usually the shade of a falkai's underbelly, pinkened, and her eyes flashed at me. But she didn't deny it.

"Ah. There is no shame in a healthy fear of something that endangers you," I said. "But now that I understand, I will not push you." I paused and watched her shoulders relax a half-stret, as she had turned away from me again. "However, I will endeavor to increase the speed with which I travel the passageway. If I double it, I daresay you could manage."

"I appreciate your offer," she said, her voice quiet. "But it won't be necessary."

"Very well, debt-mate," I said. "I'll leave you to your work."

"Thank you," she said, her words sounding like they were bitten off rather than spoken.

Removing my helmet and armor once more, I dove into the water and swam as fast as I could, navigating the turns with ease, my body an arrow in the liquid. Had today's patrol ended normally, I would even now be at my vacation home, similarly engaged, diving the tropical waters in search of my favorite meal, the falkai. Half my length, it could only be found during the summer season, when its scales were dropping, and it sought warmer waters near the surface. Such fish I could catch with my claws and teeth, but I preferred using my handmade spear. Of a summer night I could be found on the shore, cooking the falkai and sipping a brouka as the moon set over the horizon.

But now I timed myself speeding through an underground water channel whilst pondering our next course of action. It may be that we played a dangerous game of Snout with the Kezti. Who would turn their head first? The Kezti could no more live on Hestra's Handmaid than could the humans. When they failed to find Shay, (and myself), they would be forced to leave at the arrival of Hestra's winter.

I reached the shore where the pool stopped and rose out of the water, noting the huge cavern and its several openings of varying size. Pausing to listen, I focused my attention. It would not do to successfully navigate the channel only to land in the hands of the enemy lying in wait.

But all was quiet, and no Kezti smells invaded my nostrils. Dipping below the water, I sped back the way I came, determined to beat my time but also crafting other possible solutions.

When I returned to our cave, Shay was driving one of the long-range rifles into a back wall. Curious, I approached, water dripping off me with every step. I stopped behind her, waiting for her to speak. I'd seen her shoulders tense at my approach, so I knew she knew I was there.

"These long guns are practical," she said. "Did they intend for them to have many uses?"

"I don't know," I said. "I've only used them as guns."

"Well," she said as she grunted and pushed the weapon into the rock. "I've managed to create two bore holes. I can place my Short Bursts inside a couple dismantled Galvanite tubes, and we can hang back in the opposite corner. They're

Short Bursts which mean we don't need a large blast radius, but if you're more comfortable, you can submerge in the pool. But I don't anticipate any problems. This is all standard iron ore and gangue that I've been retreat mining for the last three revolutions."

"What will these Short Bursts do?" I said and stepped closer as she withdrew the long gun and leaned it against the rock wall.

"The charges will initiate a limited shock wave, weakening the existing fractures in this wall, as well as volumizing any gaps that exist in the collapsed tunnel which is adjacent to my bore holes."

Shay's helmet translated but I tilted my head, not catching every meaning.

"To simplify, I'm going to create another collapse, but it will be controlled," she said. She pointed to the slope of the ground from where we stood. "If my math is right, the rock fall should flow this direction. As long as this blast does what it's supposed to, I can duplicate it on the other side, and it should open up a path right to where we were before the Kezti dropped their bomb."

"Hoom," I said and turned to look at the water. "Is there a possibility the rock fall would fill the cave pool and block our exit that way?"

Shay's mouth thinned, and she averted her gaze once more.

Tightness in my own chest threatened to erupt in an angry accusation, but I remembered her skin, so delicate under my rough hands. I remembered her frantic plashing in the water in her efforts to turn when she felt she was running out of air.

"Will you allow a day-cycle for us to consider all options?" I said at last, using the tone I saved for addressing my sister's offspring, a brood of hellions I oft avoided at length.

"That's fair," she said and unlatched her helmet. Her hair stuck to her hairline with sweat, and she exhaled, walking away with her helmet under her arm. She removed her "Core Suit" and a second layer of clothes as well as her foot coverings and lowered herself into the water.

I amended my assessment. She wasn't afraid of the water. She was afraid of not being able to come up for air.

Determined to attempt the route again, I decided to leave off replacing my armor, but now I would rest. And perhaps admire Shay's strange, defenseless body as she dipped her head under and spread her fingers through her hair. I liked how it floated in the water akin to the sea fronds the falkai hid themselves in. Perhaps I would get another chance to touch her; my fingers burned to know what those shining filaments felt like twining about them.

Chapter 19

I stayed under water for as long as I could, trying and failing to get the heat from my cheeks to cool. I hadn't felt this ashamed or embarrassed in over a decade. Drail's innocent question shone a spotlight on my fear and desperation.

He was right.

We had a viable way out with a little more effort on my part. If I miscalculated, I could seal us even tighter inside this cave and turn it into a mausoleum.

Was I really going to let my fear of drowning overtake my good sense? In the mining community, we often talked about how the veterans were just as likely, if not moreso, to die in senseless accidents as rookies. Rookies came to the jobsite with caution that had been grav-chiseled into their heads. Veterans could become complacent after so many years of work without any accidents. It was the caution that prevented the accidents, not the experience.

Coming up for air, I turned my head enough to see that Drail watched me in the water, and I shivered.

Replaying my sentences in my mind, I felt my cheeks heat again. *"If" my math is right. The rock fall "should" flow this way. "As long as" the blast does what it's supposed to. It "should" open a path.* I was talking about detonating explosives in a chamber no bigger than the gym on the *Dynamo's* Rec Deck. Yes, they were Short Bursts. Yes, I did the math that showed the most probable blast dynamics. But there was no feasible way to guarantee our safety with a hundred percent certainty. Unlike the Room and Pillar mines my team and I had been clearing, this chamber didn't have two escape routes or any blast shields.

Crawling out of the water once more, I missed my colorful throw blanket and mug of hot tea. Aw hell. I missed a lot of stuff.

Still avoiding Drail's eyes, I combed my fingers through my hair to get most of the tangles out and tied it up into a ponytail again. I wrapped my arms around my knees and let my head tip back, as if I was soaking up the rays of the sun and not wishing a fissure would open up in the ground and swallow me whole.

The softest whisper of noise fluttered behind me, and then Drail was there. He placed his long legs at either side of mine and cocooned me with his warm body, resting his arms on his legs, but close enough at my back that I could feel the thrum of his heartbeat and slow, even breaths.

God, it felt amazing to be warm.

I trembled, but not from the chill air anymore. Drail was a mammoth heated blanket, and he was just what I needed in this moment.

Mulling over what I should say, I bit my lip. I should acknowledge how he was right to ask his question. Admit it was a dangerous idea best left for a desperate last resort. But I felt warm and sleepy. And we couldn't understand each other anyway if we talked; we needed at least one helmet within hearing distance. And it felt like he scooched a teensy bit closer behind me. And, and, and.

Chapter 20

Assuring my debt-mate's comfort took precedence over all else. It was both my duty and my honor. My fellow Svaitans would frown upon anything less. I had made peace with my new responsibilities.

These were my thoughts as I surrounded Shay's body with my own, creating a shelter at her back. It mattered not that she only wore scant bits of fabric molded to her strange, smooth skin, or that her saturated hair purified her scent until the entire cave smelled of Shay Leviticus.

Stretting closer but not close enough to touch, I sensed her body heat mingling with mine as the water droplets evaporated from her skin. I had yet to understand her body's thermoregulation. When she was angered, her body temperature rose. When blood rushed to her face from embarrassment or interest, it likewise rose. It seemed her emotions controlled her temperature unlike the Svai. We controlled our own temperature as it suited us, with glands under our arms as easily manipulated as the muscles attached to our eyelids.

As Shay faced the dark and still cave pool, I let my gaze roam over what I could see of her. Pale leg skin, ten tiny digits extended from her feet, knees criss-crossed with lighter scars, as well as her hands and arms; the network of white lines slashing every which way denoted numerous cuts and lacerations across a long span of time. Again, I silently quested the human Creators—why create children with a skin covering so fragile as to be scraped by the simplest rock or tool?

Studying my own thick scales, I contrasted their dark color and rough texture to Shay's arms mere strets from mine. All I need do was lift my hands from my legs and cross them over Shay's body, bringing her within my embrace. Then I would press my chest to her back and feel her life force steady against mine. But she warmed without my touch; it wouldn't do to infringe upon her personal space. A thought jerked my attention back to my arms so close to hers. Would my skin abrade hers?

But Shay sank against me without warning, and I realized she'd fallen asleep. Looking down at her bared neck, I could see tendons and the place her blood tunnel pulsed. Her head rested against my lower chest, and the spill of yellow filaments brushed my skin.

It was imperative I hold her. That she would not bend uncomfortably as a matter of course. With gentle strength, I gathered her in my arms and cradled her head at my shoulder, and she sighed in her sleep then nuzzled against me, though my hide couldn't be dissimilar from the very cave walls that surrounded us.

But she slept on, and if I smoothed my hands along the scars on her arms, what of it? It was my honor-bound duty to ensure the wellbeing of my debt-mate. And I learned for myself that the powerful scales of the Svai did not abrade supple human skin.

The deep purring rumble of contentment rolled from within my chest, and yet another thought seized my attention and would not relent its grip. I could never be content again without Shay Leviticus at my side.

I would sleep for a quarter span, but then I knew what I must do while she rested.

Chapter 21

I couldn't help the long sigh of refreshment I exhaled as I stretched and woke up, blinking in the pale light emitted by my helmet. I hadn't slept that soundly in a month of cycles. Pushing up from the smooth ground, I realized I'd slept in my jump shorts and sports bra. My Core Suit and NorClimb layers lay folded by my helmet; I hadn't dressed after my quick bath and Drail—my *debt-mate*—had taken it upon himself to be my personal dryer. And possibly scaly duvet? I remembered nodding off, feeling safer and cozier than I had in revolutions. Maybe in forever.

But where was he now?

Scanning the cavern's dark corners, I could see he wasn't here, which meant he was in the cave pool. He hadn't overruled my plan outright, although he would have been within his rights and sensible had he done so. Rather he'd suggested we think about it, and he'd also declared his intention to swim fast enough that he could take me with him before I ran out of air.

Not knowing when he left for his practice run, I decided to eat, squat in a far corner, don my Core Suit, and organize my supplies and weapons. A cursory glance into the bag holding the planet engine showed everything was as it should be. The long gun bore holes were surprisingly the exact diameter that would house one of the engine tubes, which would make them ideal for tamping the Short Bursts inside. But that would mean releasing the Outer Gas as well as the small vials of Dark Miasma from two of them. The Outer Gas was harmless and would dissipate into the cave air and the cave pool, leaving a faint trace of itself. The vial of Dark Miasma would stay with me, of course, but without the Galvanite rods and carefully measured ratio of Outer Gas, the planet engine would cease to be.

Perhaps it was for the best.

If Granda found us, *me*, then the engine was compromised, and I was as good as dead.

Every cell in my body resisted the idea of destroying it, though.

I'd been so close to true freedom.

Set for life.

Sighing, I zipped up that bag and focused on restocking my suit's pockets with supplies. Every item had its own pocket, making it easier to access what I needed, like when I'd had to rappel down to secure Drail.

Next, I cleaned and reassembled my weapons. Too bad we couldn't use the Entropy Gun to blast a new tunnel, but it had its limitations. A glass wall with four boundaries was a simple matter for the disintegrating pulse to eliminate, but meters' thick rock walls had no clear boundaries. I'd just as soon not guess what the disintegrating pulse would do inside a cave.

A splash broke the stillness of the cave, and Drail climbed out, heaving. He wasn't usually so winded; he must have pushed himself.

"Are you alright?" I asked, and he looked at me with a small smile before collapsing to the rock. I rushed to him and knelt at his side, seeing bloodied knuckles on his hands, broken claws, and on closer inspection, lacerations on his ridge brows and the top if his head.

His chest rose and fell, but he didn't answer me, and I ran my hands along his body looking and feeling for more injuries. Had the Kezti dropped another bomb? But I hadn't felt anything. Eyes darting to the water, I half-expected our enemies to emerge, but the ripples were already ebbing. Leaning over his legs, I saw that his clawed feet also bore cuts and scrapes as well as broken claws.

Confused and worried, I returned to caress Drail's brow.

"Hey," I said, my voice soft. I petted his face and let my fingers trace his jaw and knuckles brush the tender, vulnerable skin at his throat. "Drail. Debt-mate."

Watching his eyes, I rested my hand over where I thought his heart might be. His eyelids fluttered, and opening slowly, they blinked at me while he licked his thin lips with that long, black tongue of his.

"This must be made into a ritual of awakening," he said as he grasped my hand and brought it to his mouth. His nostrils flared as he smelled each of my fingers and then licked my palm; I laughed and tried to pull my hand back, but his grip tightened. "Nay, I have use for this." He spread my fingers using his thumb and then placed my hand at his throat. "Stroke it as you did before," he said, his voice brooking no argument.

Surprised at his audacity, I obeyed him anyway.

"What happened to you?" I whispered even as I continued to smooth my hand up and down his throat as he lifted his chin for greater access.

"It required much time," he said, his speech causing the skin at his throat to vibrate under my fingers. "And only the iron hide and colossal strength of a Svai could accomplish it." He moaned when I used both hands to caress his throat. "But

I created two pockets of air along the tunnel by pounding mercilessly against the rock. You may safely traverse the channel to its exit."

Biting my lip, I let my hands pause their ministrations. "I guess you didn't trust my math," I said, forcing a chuckle.

Drail groaned and sat up, securing my hands in his and leaning forward to run his snout around my helmet. "Can you not transfer the translation software to your wrist unit, that we might communicate without these hindrances?" He drew back and looked at me, still holding my hands in his bloody ones. "I cannot smell you properly. But nay. I trust my life with you in all things. Nevertheless, I felt it a travesty to destroy your planet engine and rathered a few bruised knuckles in exchange. I trust my solution is more than satisfactory. Superior, in fact."

My vision blurred as I pulled my hands out of his grasp and unfastened my helmet. It clattered to the ground as I tackled the gigantic Drail and drove him back to the ground, burying my face in the place between his soft throat and rough shoulder. "It's perfect," I said and sighed when I felt his snout meander through my hair and along my neck.

He mumbled things I didn't understand but then licked the skin at my throat, and I felt his teeth graze along my jaw. This was it, then. This was how I died on Mining Planet. Devoured by a handsome, smug and boastful glorified lizard—who happened to respect my dreams and work as much as he respected me.

Chapter 22

We took leave of our senses even as I took Shay's fabric layers from her body. She had no need of them; my heated muscular frame would provide warmth, as would our sexual exploits, I had no doubt.

Judging by the aroma wafting from her neck, the human female was amenable to my attentions. Additionally, she aided me in removing the more stubborn of her coverings.

Gasping at the sight of her scaleless skin, part of me wished to cover it once more, perhaps even in armor, lest she endure more cuts or scrapes that would mar its perfection. But my nostrils flared and mouth watered even as my *pilo* sensors alerted me to chemical changes in the air.

Two mounds of buff flesh with darker skin at their points beckoned with a unique scent of their own, a concentrated version of what I'd come to associate with Shay Leviticus, and I lay her upon her large coat to protect her back while I feasted at the table of her exposed body. At her side, I sniffed around the fleshy mounds and heard Shay whine before she grabbed my face and pulled me down to her chest.

"Tell me what you desire," I growled, but she wouldn't know what I asked.

When she cupped one mound and angled my mouth towards it, I took that to mean she intended for me to explore with greater intensity, and I obeyed my debt-mate's command. Swirling my tongue about the incredibly soft skin that gave at the slightest pressure, I kneaded both of them with care, mesmerized by their movement, their texture, their taste, and most especially, the sounds Shay made when I attended to them.

How did she react to a tentative caress? Writhing as a wave of tiny colorless bumps rippled along her skin.

What sounds did she make when I cupped and squeezed? Moans and pleas. I snuck a glance at her face and saw her dark eyes intent on me. She licked her lips.

In a moment of inspiration, I was moved upon to suckle one of the globes, and Shay's reaction gratified me such that I employed the technique with vigor, switching between the two with delight and wonder. My cock extruded amidst my tasting, but I paid it no mind. I never imagined tasting an alien female in this way, but now I found I couldn't stop.

Now my hands were traveling the length of her body—a body susceptible to countless injuries, but I traced her skin with care, tracking my claws along her muscles and leaving a wake of more curious tiny bumps and my mistress's hitching gasps of breath.

"An entire body covered in skin as sensitive as that of my throat," I murmured, watching her face while I glided my hands back and forth. Her brows met; her cheeks, throat and chest flushed; her eyes darkened.

With rumbling deep in my chest, my breaths accelerated, and my focus honed on the woman. She was a light in this dark cave, and I longed to communicate. Tell her of her beauty. Her mysterious hold on me by sheer virtue of her intelligence and courage.

Where my claws went my tongue followed, and I delved it into the crease at the juncture of her thighs; it was thus with the females of my race, but her flavor differed, its light saltiness a contrast to the sweet juices she produced as I explored her fascinating and delicate innermost folds. Her voice spoke gentle commands and earnest pleadings, and I did my best to interpret it, aided by her subtle movements and forceful direction with her hands.

When I discovered the hidden bead that would unleash my debt-mate's pleasure, I tread that holy ground with care. Slow licks, deep nuzzles, and the probing finger of which one claw was ground down by the rock, all combined to cause Shay's body to undulate in a rhythm designed to stoke my own desire to flaming embers.

"Is this done in your race?" I asked after lifting my head to see her expressions. She appeared in a daze but smiled when she met my eyes.

"Pleezdohntztahp," she said, but what did it mean? I withdrew my thick finger, and she frowned and lifted her pelvis. "Nononono!"

Chuckling, I slid my finger back in place, and she calmed.

Grunting, I smiled and returned my attention to the soft mat of curls and the heated, slick skin between her legs.

Growling into her cleft, I continued lashing her bead with my tongue while thrusting my finger into her, watching her face with eager hunger out of the corner of my eye. My tail had roamed along her body while I was at my work, and it circled her mounds and swiped at her gasping mouth, exploring every soft curve and indentation, until I willed it to join my finger. It swirled around it inside of her, and judging by her gasping whimpers, it enhanced her pleasure. Her flavor and scent overwhelmed me, and I squeezed my eyes shut in bliss, plunging into her while dancing with her arousal, forward and back, in and out, my *pilo* sensors alert for the miniscule changes that would announce my debt-mate's climax.

By Svai's Design, my very heart thundered in time to our pulsing chant, and I thought if the Svai could cry, then surely my emotions would now overtake my eyes and produce water. I sighed and growled, licking at my leisure until her movements intensified.

Creaminess coated my finger and tail tip, and I knew Shay would be able to accept me, if not with ease, at least with slipperiness. My sensors tingled in a rush, racing along my neck and shoulders, and then Shay burst around me in gasping pleas, her body shuddering and hands clutching at my head and shoulder where she could reach, and I chuckled while continuing my tongue's assault.

She laughed and squirmed out of reach, saying words in her lilting language but then grabbing my swollen cock, and I stilled.

Her panting quieted, and my mating instinct bade me snarl when I met her languid gaze with my narrowed eyes. For a microspan, I saw the fragile human as prey and licked my teeth. A growl reverberated around the cave and my mouth watered. I lunged at her, teeth bared, but when they met the soft skin at her shoulder, I caught myself before biting. Holding my breath, I waited.

When I raised my head, she smiled at me, her eyes softening at the corners, and I straddled her, taking care to nuzzle her neck and breathe deep of her innocent scent while I tamed the feral beast that would take without mercy.

The females of the Svai were as ferocious and formidable as the males and our race mated in a frenzy of blood, our jaws anchoring in the tough hides of our nestmates. As clever and courageous as Shay was, she would not survive such a coupling.

Assured of her wetness and enthusiasm, I stopped and looked into her dark eyes before inhaling the fragrance at her neck and jaw, swiping at her lips with my tongue, and shivering when she ran her nose along my neck.

Positioning my cock at her entrance, I gulped air at the sensation of tunneling into her at the pace of running sap, so slowly that time stopped, and her warmth swallowed me by degrees until I was fully seated.

Her voice husky, she murmured precious words and then wrapped her bare ankles around my thighs and pulled against them while arching her back.

Holding still, I felt my member throb inside her. Was she in pain?

Thrashing her head, she moaned and then grabbed at my chest with her hands, trying to pull me close. I leaned closer, feeling the heat between us intensify as my desire to move, to glide, to *pound*, threatened to consume me. But perhaps humans did not employ such tactics?

Shay frowned, her voice low when she spoke as if threatening me. She wanted—no, demanded—something of me. But what?

Grasping my hips with her hands, she forced the smallest push-pull motion and groaned, and I quivered with ecstasy. It appeared my debt-mate wanted the same thing that I did.

A proper fucking.

Staring into her eyes, I pulled out slowly until she looked like she would assassinate me—and then I plowed deep, retreating and advancing with witless abandon, watching as relief and then pleasure suffused her face. Her cries echoed about the chamber.

"Chamron falls!" I shouted, her eagerness overcoming my caution, and I continued rutting, the tendons in my neck straining as my hips worked in tandem with her own ambition.

Where I would have waited, she strove; where I would have slowed, she raced, and when I rumbled my pleasure deep in my chest, she moaned and clenched my hips with her fragile fingers and grunted more words. What could I do but follow her direction?

She hadn't minded my tail's attentions earlier, so I treated her hindquarters as I would a Svai female and used my tail to tease her other orifice, hearing Shay squeak and whimper from shock then pleasure. Her moans escalated until her keening cry sounded throughout the cave. Smug, I grinned as I approached the apex of our mating.

Fires in my belly and blood ignited, and I roared my pleasure-spill, licking Shay's mouth after I emptied my seed into her womb, and then I rolled onto my back with her, holding her close to my heart and frantically petting her skin wherever I could reach, marveling at the sensation of pliable, smooth skin beneath hands as textured as tree bark, and inhaling the scent of her musk and sweat just beneath her ear and at the pulse in her throat, and under her arms and between her shoulders and neck, and at the crown of her head. Flooding my nostrils and my *pilo* sensors with her essence until she permeated me as thoroughly as if I'd been dipped in a bath of it.

She kissed my throat, and I groaned, but then she pressed her mouth all over my face, cheeks, closed eyes, snout and mouth, devouring me with the ferocity of a spring breeze, and I laughed.

She joined me but reached over and snagged her helmet, putting it on so we could communicate. We both looked down at her sprawling, exposed body and laughed again. She spoke.

"I don't have words," she said, breathless, shaking her head.

"Then why did you don your helmet?"

She chuckled and sat up, and my brows rose at the sight of her glistening flesh mounds, especially where the darkened tips pearled.

"I desire to taste these once more," I said and tweaked them with my hands.

"You're a boob man, huh?" she said.

"Boob?" I repeated.

"Oh, do your females not have breasts?" she asked.

"Nay," said and sighed when Shay stroked the skin at my throat with erotic caresses.

"Let me guess," she said, one of her brows raising to mirror my own expression. "Your babies are born with teeth and claws and can crawl right away?"

"Of course," I said with a scoff. "I should not be surprised if you tell me that human young are even more weak and defenseless than the adults."

Shay shook her head. "Well. For the record, let it be known that this lowly human is very grateful that a superior specimen such as yourself deigned to have sex with me." She leaned forward and pressed her breasts over my face, making sure to plump them together with her hands and caress my throat with them until I begged for mercy.

"What is a boob man?" I asked, my eyes narrowing on the dark tips that were mere strets from my mouth.

"A male who can't get enough breasts," she murmured. "Which are also known as boobs or tits."

Growling, I lengthened my tongue to swirl around her *tits* with fervor.

She threw her head back, and I grinned, trilling my pleasure in the back of my throat.

"Oooh, that's a new sound," she said with glee. "I have a confession to make, Drail."

"I'm listening."

"I'm suddenly extremely happy to be your debt-mate, and I plan to save your life regularly, so you'll be stuck with me forever," she said. Her smile had sobered, and her eyes shone as she placed her open palm over my heart. "I'm actually really serious about this."

Nodding, I covered her hand with mine.

"I, too, came to this conclusion, mate of my heart," I said. "I can no longer conceive of an existence without you by my side."

She smiled.

"Whew," she said, her lips pursing. "I was a little nervous you wouldn't feel the same way."

"I would expect an inferior race such as yours to be in a constant state of anxiety," I said, waiting to see her eyes darken with a gleam of irritation before I chuckled and continued. "But after this rousing span of such fine sexual sport, how could I not? Truly, Svai's Design is greater than even I could have wished. We have but to conquer our enemies, and then we may pursue your lofty schemes to pilot planets across the universe."

Her smile glowed, and I vowed in my heart to do all in my power to preserve this precious life. But perhaps my vow was inconsequential. The tally grew in her favor with each passing day-span. I remained hopelessly in Chamron's ledger, but though my balance grew in debt, I found I could not regret a moment of it. He may be the God of debt and wanting, but the more I owed to the odd human, the less I lacked.

Chapter 23

Bathed, fed, and dressed, we strategized how best to ferry Drail's armor, the long guns, and my bags. I disliked the decision but reluctantly agreed it made the most sense for Drail to make two trips before I joined him for his third. He insisted it was nearly effortless. Watching the muscles in his back bunch as he knifed through the water with his second load, I believed him.

What I didn't believe was that I felt such a bond with someone from an alien race. Something prevented me from naming it love; probably plain old pragmatism. We didn't know each other from the genesis of the universe, but there was a steadiness between us. Could it be as simple as that? We had an undefinable peace when we were together. And God, the sex. I'd be lying if I said I wasn't excited to engage in "such fine sexual sport" again, as Drail called it. I smiled so wide my cheeks hurt. What a guy.

Sealing my last water pouch, I zipped it up tight in one of my thigh suit pockets with a satisfied pat. Sitting by the water, my leg bounced of its own volition.

Waiting for his return had me on edge. It was like watching those drama vids where the happy family all smiled at each other in the shuttle right before a meteor wiped them out. Chewing my nails, I recognized that old anxiety rear its head again. It'd been my constant companion in my early childhood. Walking on eggshells around my aunt. Learning to pickpocket in New Capetown just so we'd have enough money to buy a small loaf of bread and a yam. There had been precious little joy back then, and anything I'd managed to scrounge up, like the one-eyed kitten or my childhood friend Petro, had faded away before my happiness had time to flourish.

Picking the pocket of Dr. Eli Nkosi had been the first glimmer of hope in a dark world. It turned out he knew all about me. Not literally. He'd grown up in similar circumstances, but after he won the sponsorship of a caring adult, he'd become Earth's leading environmental physicist during the Accountability Years. And walking the mean streets of New Capetown that evening, he'd been in the right place at the right time. Setting me on a course of academic success, he'd been my literal savior. His death right before I began engineering school had almost crushed me.

Shaking off the melancholy, I swiped at the tear on my cheek and exhaled. I knew what the problem was.

Caring for someone opened the door for tremendous pain. It'd been simple to barge into danger's way and rescue Drail from the Kezti. I didn't know him. It just seemed like the right thing to do.

But now?

Now we faced some shit odds, if I was honest. And now I cared about him.

The object of my affection broke the surface of the cave pool and pulled himself up beside me. Our helmets had been packed in my duffel bags in hopes of preserving the internal electronics. I'd managed to partially download the translation software into my WU as Drail had suggested, but without a way to charge it, the download lagged and fizzled out.

"Ready?" I asked, waiting to see if my wrist unit would catch it.

Drail smiled his wicked smile and nodded, and I dropped into the water, feeling strange with my Core Suit and grippers on. We paddled to the rock wall where the water disappeared into the channel, and I took a deep breath and dove down where Drail grasped me around the waist and then swam with insane speed. Before I knew it, he'd slowed and nudged me up. I reached up and felt my fingers break the surface and touch rock a few inches above.

Lungs tight, I approached the air well and took a satisfying breath, then dipped below the water again where Drail could whisk me through the water to the last spot. A final deep breath, and down I went again, the eerie underwater channel skating by in a blur as my wrist unit's delicate glow lit the cloudy water.

Drail's primordial mining method had doubtless introduced a lot of rock dust. Just how much abuse could his body take?

We sped along until Drail lifted me with him up into a huge chamber that echoed when we splashed and gasped for air.

Our helmets sat beside our bags in a neat pile, two beacons of light.

We climbed out and sat, arms resting on our knees while water dripped from fingertips—and claws.

"Thank you," I said, feeling my face heat when I gave him a shy smile. Which made no sense. The man had nosed his way into my most private parts, seen and touched and tasted every centimeter of me.

"I am but observing my duty to my debt-mate," he said with an affected accent and stately bow.

Quirking a brow, I stared at him.

His feral grin split his scaly face and he chucked my chin with a knuckle.

"Get you your maps," he said. "Let us plot a scheme."

I took a deep breath and nodded, fishing one out of my bag's side pocket along with its companion grease pencil.

"We can't know exactly what they've decimated until we surface," I said, scouring the map that showed the base. I exed out the comms towers and the living quarters. "What's the range of one of their Renegade bombs?"

Drail studied the map and asked for the other one that showed sublevels. "Where does this tunnel correspond to the base?" His claw tapped where we'd cowered under an archway.

"Okay. That's over here, this empty field to the west of the S&R bays," I said.

"Ah. The Kezti Renegade bomb disperses at a decastret above ground, sending out a radial burst of mini-bombs before its main ball detonates just below ground level," he said, borrowing my pencil and circling a diameter of roughly twenty meters in the area I'd pointed to. "Without knowing what the Kezti believe they will be doing with this planet, I cannot say with confidence where they would strike. But perhaps they would wish to preserve some of the profitable infrastructure. And the blast we felt in the tunnels reflected an approximation of an impact here, factoring in the depth of rock."

"That makes sense," I said. Scrutinizing the base once more, I found the sole surface building that sat above the Hub. "I'm guessing this is gone. I forgot about the first blast we felt when we were in the engine room."

"Hoom. And what of the elevator this Granda entity mentioned?"

I scowled.

"The secret elevator I had to learn about from a computer," I said. "Well, the engine room isn't directly below the Hub but rather several meters this way. The elevator would have to be located ... here."

We looked at the base map and saw a collection of outbuildings.

"Granda would have told the Kezti to leave that area alone, I'm guessing," I said. "Everything revolves around the planet engine." I sat back and looked at Drail who had put his armor back on save his helmet. I was glad. I much preferred seeing his dear face and beautiful grass-green eyes. "I think Granda planned to waltz into the engine room, take me by surprise, commandeer the engine, and steal MP-13 out from under IGMC's nose with the Kezti pirates acting as an escort out of this star system."

"If that is so," Drail said, "then he would not care what the Kezti obliterated in their attempts to flush you out of the tunnels."

"Right." I tapped the pencil against the base map and bit my lip, my eyes glazing over as I tried to anticipate what Granda's next move would be. "He can't steal the planet without me or the engine. He can't find me, yet. And he can't stay on MP-13 indefinitely. How patient are the Kezti?"

Drail huffed a laugh. "The Kezti do not have a word for patient. Does that answer your question?"

I took off my helmet, wanting fresh air. Hopefully my wrist unit could keep up with the conversation. "So Granda is under duress," I said, absently tracing my lips with a finger until Drail captured my hand and nuzzled into my palm.

"Allow me," he said, and trailed a claw along my bottom lip. "Perhaps the mighty Svai lack an aspect or two that could improve our way of life."

"Like what?" I asked, smiling at his distraction.

"Fleshy lips such as you possess," he said, his gaze fixated on where his claw pressed into my bottom lip. "And of course, tits."

"Of course," I said with a chuckle and took his hand, kissing his palm and pressing my cheek into it. I sighed. "I don't think we can wait him out, as impatient as the Kezti must be."

Drail rolled his shoulders. "You are right. He will grow desperate by the span and let us not forget the Svai and the Kezti are locked in battle somewhere above Hestra."

"Depending on what exactly he promised the pirates," I said, searching Drail's face. "He could send hundreds of them into the tunnels."

Drail returned my gaze and dipped his head. He stroked my fingers and inner wrists and traced the network of scars on the backs of my hands. "So vulnerable to injury. And yet so fiery and resolute."

"What do you mean?" I asked, mesmerized by the delicate touch of claws he'd used to grip into the very rock of this planet against my skin.

"I can see the thoughts behind your brown-stone eyes," he said, looking at me with a sad expression. "You plan to bait Marsel Granda into capturing you, so that you may best him in close combat."

I caught my breath and averted my eyes for a second. Breathed deep and met his eyes once more.

"But will you help me?"

He cracked his neck and blinked two sets of lids, then bared his teeth. Furrowing his brow ridge, he peered at me.

"How else am I to save your life and pay my debt? I will help you."

The tremors in my chest calmed to a gentle flutter, and I realized he hadn't rolled his shoulders.

Snatching my pencil back, I circled a small box.

"I need to get here."

Chapter 24

Nay, I did not like Shay's plan, nor her bravery, nor her stubbornness. But I respected and admired her spirit, and as her debt-mate, I was in no place to assert my superiority. I had not saved her life thrice within a day-cycle or two.

And so it was I hid in the shadows while my small woman stood at the door of a nondescript metal outbuilding with the black planet engine bag slung over her shoulder and knocked.

I heard muffled speaking, and the door slid open; she stepped inside. The door slid shut, and my debt-mate disappeared from my view.

I scowled at the ugly metal buildings, the black rocky dust at my boots, and the blasted rubble scattered about the base without rhyme or reason. For now, the planetoid was not besieged by scores of Kezti pirates.

By Svai's Design, if my mate did not return to me …

But that was nonsense. Upon my honor I was bound to protect her, and I would.

Shay Leviticus was not the only stubborn entity on Hestra's Handmaid.

Baring my teeth in an unholy grin, I devised an addendum to Shay's carefully crafted plan. It would not interfere. Much.

Chapter 25

Acting on a hunch, I spoke the same password for the "Captain's elevator" as was used to access the engine room's computer, and the door slid open. I couldn't look back at Drail because if I did, I knew I'd run to him and lose my nerve.

He wouldn't mind rescuing me; I knew this. But this situation wasn't something I could be rescued from. I had to do it, and I had to do it on my terms.

A screen inside the elevator showed basic MP-13 stats as well as the levels it was zipping past. Comms were marked as "offline", as well as Power Bank Turbine 2. That's where one of their bombs landed. Everything else was labeled "Low Energy Output".

As the elevator descended, my gut churned, and my mouth dried up. Rehearsing my plans for the twentieth time in my head, I tried to convince myself it was going to work.

The first problem was not knowing exactly where the Captain's elevator opened. I knew the engine room inside and out; how could I have missed an actual elevator door? But considering it had been kept secret from me, of course it wasn't going to be obvious.

When it stopped, the door slid open, and I stepped into an unlit corridor. Of course. The decoy hallway.

I was about to head up the hall when I heard the thudding steps of a Kezti pirate.

Tucking back into the elevator and crouching in the small dark space, I waited for it to pass, thankful the elevator's status screen had darkened. With luck, the Kezti wouldn't notice the dark opening. Its steps continued until it reached the door to the "auxiliary storage". I heard the beeping of the security panel and the snick of the door sliding open. Granda had given the Kezti the code.

Keeping my breathing soft and steady, I listened as the Kezti moved things around in the room. Then its stomping gait as it returned up the corridor. I held my breath as it passed and noted the faint gleam of gold as it carried one of the treasures. If they were going to empty the entire auxiliary storage room, it was going to take all day.

When its footfalls quieted, I poked my head out into the hall. All clear. A new idea had formed, and I didn't hesitate.

Sprinting down to the storage room, I ducked into it and waited beside the door.

When Drail and I had hiked from the cave's water channel to the nearest mined tunnel, I'd snuck us through service corridors and escape chutes, avoiding cameras and scattered Kezti patrols. We'd been surprised to see that the base was not, in fact, crawling with Kezti troops. Drail surmised that most of them were in aerial combat above Hestra's atmosphere engaging with the Dam Svai forces.

That meant Granda had most likely enticed the detail he'd traveled with to help themselves to the exotic valuables while he secured himself in the engine room, attempting God knows what with the computers and AGI.

But if they were collecting booty, then they weren't protecting Granda.

Steeling myself, I gripped my weapon at the sound of movement and beeping beyond the door, and then it opened.

One Kezti entered, heading straight for the mini-barrel of Krutenian honey.

I didn't hear anyone else coming, so I aimed at the pirate's slender thorax and fired; it fell in two pieces, just as Drail had said it would.

Working fast, I dragged his parts behind a huge, locked chest and returned to my hiding spot.

They didn't catch on until the third one didn't return.

I heard voices and knew the fourth had brought reinforcements. The door opened.

"How difficult is it to move some trinkets from this room to the Hub?" Marsel Granda complained from the corridor. "Your compatriots are probably lying drunk in here."

A Kezti warrior strode in followed by Granda. They stood facing the shrine I'd concocted for the purpose: drawing their undivided attention. Using loot from around the room, I'd assembled an eye-catching display of treasure surrounded by dead Kezti warriors I'd posed to look like they were worshipping at an altar.

I fired a single shot at Granda's bodyguard who fell in a heap and waited for him to turn around.

"You," he said, his voice dripping with disdain. "I lost track of you in the mines; I thought a blast got you."

"No," I said. "It didn't."

"You've caused a lot of grief," he said, taking a step toward me even though I trained my gun on him. "I had to promise the Kezti all sorts of kickbacks thanks to your shenanigans."

"One more step, and you'll save me the boredom of listening to you explain all your justifications for betraying

IGMC and the entire staff on the Dynamo and MP-13," I said, cocking my weapon so he could hear it. He stopped.

"It isn't too late, Shay," he said and raised his hands slowly. "A simple comm conversation to my Kezti contact offplanet, and you'll be reinstated as MP-13's propulsion expert."

I scoffed. "Don't tell me you passed yourself off as the propulsion expert," I said and shook my head.

"You caught me," Granda said with a lopsided smile.

Cocking my head, I frowned. Granda never smiled.

A blur out of the corner of my eye was all the warning I had to shift my weapon, but it was too late.

Captain Mear tackled me to the ground and slammed my wrist against the floor, forcing me to drop my weapon. I yelped in pain, but Granda and the captain worked quickly to fasten my wrists behind my back and drag me up the dark tunnel and around the corner to the passage that led down to the engine room.

Mear had my pack slung around his shoulder and dragged me along with ease, his face a granite block of resolve.

"This wasn't me, Mear," I said, wincing with the throb of my wrist. "I lost radio contact with Granda. I went up with the shuttle," I said, casting an agonized look at Granda's back as he strode down the tunnel. "The shuttle was shot down and when I tried to ping the Communications Officer, one of the Kezti answered. I knew *nothing* about this!"

"That was the intention," Mear said without looking at me. "You shouldn't have survived the shuttle crash."

Stunned, I pulled up short, causing Mear to trip and curse.

"What?" he said with a growl and jerked me by the collar until I stumbled forward again. "Did you think you were irreplaceable? The only one who could captain a Sphere Ship?"

Thoughts racing, I realized I'd better keep my mouth shut if I wanted to learn what was going on. 'Piloting' a Sphere Ship *did* require a propulsion engineer. It wasn't as simple as pressing a button and firing up a jet. IGMC held my contract, and I'd gone over it with a fine-toothed comb before signing. There was literally one person who could do it. Me.

We stood behind Granda as he opened the door to the engine room, and the three of us walked in. It seemed like years had passed since I'd been in here, but it had only been a couple day-cycles. With alarm I spied the rumpled bandage Drail had dropped, but neither Granda nor Mear noticed it.

They stared at the room bathed in blue light, naked without the planet engine.

Mear shook himself and grasped my elbow, pulling me to the closest chair and pushing me into it. He reconfigured my restraints to secure my wrists around the spine of the chair, then grabbed my pack from the floor where he'd set it.

"One wonders why you came back here with this," he said, black brows furrowing over his black eyes. "What is it? A decoy of some kind?" He unzipped the bag and pulled out a Galvanite rod. He slipped it back in and counted the others. "It's all here," he said, throwing me a suspicious look but handing it off to Granda.

Swallowing, I looked down at my dusty Core Suit. I hadn't anticipated Mear being with Granda, and my plan was going to shit.

Granda took the pack and marched into the blue room, quickly assembling the tesseract as each piece stabilized in its electromagnetic cradle. His movements were efficient, flawless. He'd been practicing.

"Just because you know how to put it together doesn't mean you can pilot the Sphere Ship," I said, my voice steady even though I shook inside. When did he learn to assemble it? How?

He snapped the final tube in place and stood back, admiring it as it slowly began to rotate.

"You're right, Miner 56," he said. "I won't be." He walked toward the command center and leaned over the main console, typing in codes. "Thanks, by the way," he said, glancing over at me. "Not only for bringing the engine back to its rightful place, but for taking out that little security detail. The Kezti are not a trusting bunch. I wasn't sure how I was going to get rid of them."

Sweat poured down the back of my neck, and I gritted my teeth. I needed to *think*. Staring at my dusty Core Suit, I bit my lip. When I looked back up, I saw Captain Mear staring at me.

"What?" I said, my voice emotionless.

"Why did you bring it back?" he said. He folded his arms as he stood before me, his stance menacing.

Swallowing, I looked up at him. "I thought I could convince Granda to stop. Talk some sense into him."

Muscles feathered in his swarthy cheeks as he stared me down with hard eyes. Thin-lipped and bushy-browed, he looked angry. I'd always found him to be stern, aloof, but fair. Now I realized I didn't know the man at all.

"I don't believe you," he said and leaned over me. "Granda, help me pat her down."

Granda smirked, his blue eyes narrowing as he approached. "Talk some sense into me, huh? As if being promised wealth *and* power could be reasoned out of." His soft, unscarred hands patted my sleeves, finding the pockets and emptying them. Biners clattered to the floor, the grease pencil, chewing gum, magnetic compass.

Meanwhile, Mear had squatted, slapped my legs further apart and used his large, uncalloused hands to pat down and search my pants pockets.

Throat tightening, I gritted my teeth and stared over Mears bowed head, enduring the indignity as he emptied those, too.

The waterproof map, coils of Smart rope, anchors, vitamin loaf, the miniature tesseract puzzle. My water pouch.

Licking my lips, I flared my nostrils and calmed my breathing.

Mear stood up, his knees cracking as he did so, and opened the water pouch, staring at me. I lifted my chin when he found the Short Burst charges inside.

"Bitch," Granda muttered. He'd found the detonators in my cuff pocket.

Mear stashed the Short Burst charges inside his uniform pocket and rocked back on his heels. "That makes more sense. Bring the engine as a sign of good faith," he said. "Then, blow Granda to hell. I don't blame you, Leviticus."

Granda stood beside my chair and scoffed, but I noticed he placed me between himself and the captain.

"Just a backup plan, Sir," I said. "The Kezti aren't really in a position to promise anything. I figured once Granda realized that, we might be able to come to an agreement. At the very least, maybe try to cover up the fact he'd betrayed IGMC and pretend nothing happened." I cocked my head. "But that was before I knew you were complicit with Granda and the Kezti."

Mear smirked.

"What do you know of the Kezti? You're no better than a glorified cave rat, spending a third of your life underground."

"I know they're pirates and thieves," I said. "You didn't find it suspicious they were only too happy to hump loot out of the storage room? Wouldn't an alien nation boasting wealth and power have little need of the trinkets we kept down there?"

Mear tried to cover his wince, but I caught it.

"They're not pirates," he said. "They're poised to take control over this entire sector."

"Right," I said and leaned forward as much as my restraints allowed. "By whose calculations? Because the Causeway Passage Authority is the governing body. And the Kezti have no part in it."

Mear's eyes flashed to Granda before he stepped toward me.

"What are you talking about?" His voice grated even as his face flushed.

"Oh my God," I said and sat back, craning my neck to peer at Granda for a second before meeting Mear's gaze again. "You don't know about the Causeway?" I looked back at Granda. "What the hell, Marsel? Did the Kezti come to you at the Waystation? If they're your only contacts, then you know absolutely nothing."

I couldn't help the disbelieving laugh.

"They have advanced technology," Granda said, a tremor in his voice belying his nerves.

"My God," I said again and hung my head. "That's why more troops haven't come. All this time you thought you had the backing of a powerful alien race." I shook my head. "Instead, you made a deal with what essentially amounts to a street gang in the midst of a well-policed city."

"Granda, what the fuck is she talking about?" Mear said, his voice deadly in its calm.

"They showed me vids of their cities. Their tech. Hell, they arrived in their vanguard ships," Granda said. "You've seen them."

Captain Mear's expression didn't soften. Instead, he pulled out his sidearm and shot Granda who collapsed in a heap.

I'd yelped at the shot, then cringed, squeezing my eyes shut, waiting for a round to hit me as well. My thoughts turned to Drail, and my heart ached to be in his arms again. When nothing happened, I opened one eye and saw Mear holstering his weapon. He caught my glance and smirked.

"You might be useful, yet."

"I still don't understand who you thought was going to operate the Sphere Ship," I said, gambling he wouldn't shoot me for asking.

His smirk turned into a wide smile.

"Computer, initiate Sphere Ship protocol," he said, watching for my reaction.

Confused, I tilted my head but said nothing.

"Sphere Ship protocol initiated," the female AGI said. "Running planet engine diagnostics. Planet engine parameters clean. MP-13's power at Low Energy Output. Rerouting Power Bank Turbines 1 and 3 to engine room."

Staring at Mear, I felt my heart pounding as the AGI ran through the set-up routine. This part of the process was automated.

"Assessing proximal orbital atmospheric subduction parameters in conjunction with PH-4RT in four rotational cycles," the computer announced, and I perked up. That wasn't part of the automated process.

"Adjusting MP-13's equatorial electromagnetic field to thirty-two percent. Standby."

Chills raced up and down my arms.

All of those assessments and adjustments were subjective decisions. A *person* should be making those. My gaze snapped to the engine; if I were piloting, I would be sitting at the main console monitoring MP-13's trajectory in space with constant attention to PH-4RT's gravitational pull.

Captain Mear's chuckle reverberated in the engine room.

"The look on your face," he said. Leaning against the console he folded his arms and studied me. "What have I lectured my teams about, ad nauseum, Shay Leviticus?"

Shoulders slumping, I sighed and looked away, choosing instead to stare at the mesmerizing rotation of the planet engine. "The necessity of redundancy."

"That's why IGMC insisted on the installation of the AGI in the engine room," he said. "Did you think you were going to live forever?"

"Of course not," I said. "They were going to give me a team."

"Well, the Sphere Ship no longer needs a team," he said. "Now, tell me about this Causeway and how you know about it."

Chapter 26

My addendum was simple; call in reinforcements.

"Translator, will you talk to me? It is I, Drail," I said in my helmet, hoping Shay's computer would hear and understand.

"Hello Drail," the computer's voice said in my language. "How may I be of service to you?"

"Ah, sound blessings and bright stars," I said. "Shay Leviticus, my debt-mate, has put herself in a dangerous situation with regard to the planet engine and those who would usurp her rightful place at its helm. I recall your inability to allow humans to befall harm, and I have reason to believe the one called Marsel Granda intends to cause Shay great harm. I beseech your aid in this matter."

"Very well," the voice said. "I will see what I can do."

"You have my gratitude, Translator."

The voice didn't reply, but I trusted it as much as I could. The Code of Debt required I make use of every channel possible to aid and protect my debt-mate, this included debasing myself to ask for help, and I did it without regret. But then I must exhaust my own abilities, as well. Just as I bloodied my powerful hands to create air pockets for Shay, so too would I sacrifice my body in all other ways required.

Shay had confided the codes I might need to access various places around Hestra's Handmaid, so I crouched in my hiding spot and tried to determine where my help would be most useful.

My debt-mate was a most resourceful woman; as much as I desired to crash into the engine room and come to her aid, such hastiness could put her in harm's way or worse, myself. Then she would be forced to save my life again, thus ensuring my eternal servitude. My dark chuckle thrummed in my chest.

No, for now, I would secure our passage off the Handmaid.

Peering around the corner of the partially collapsed building to the north of the Captain's elevator entrance, I sought out a clear view to the shuttle docks. I pulled out my binoculars and zoomed in. No Kezti patrolled the ships, of which there were only two.

I remembered four Kezti had disembarked along with the short human; I did not recall a second ship landing when Shay and I were closeted in the engine room.

Vanguard ships supported up to ten Kezti warriors.

Fear seized my chest. Perhaps I should go to the engine room?

But no, Shay Leviticus was possessed of inner strength and courage. The opportunity to steal one of their ships was ripe.

Determined in my chosen course of action, I steeled myself for the trek across blasted open area.

"Translator, if you are not otherwise occupied, I would ask you to hide my activities from the monitoring station in the engine room," I spoke in my helmet.

"Very well, Drail of the Dam Svai."

I ran from blasted pile of rubble to blasted pile of rubble. Stopping to crouch and scan my surroundings at each juncture, I still saw no Kezti patrols. My Chak Dam Jai would not communicate with me at this point in time. I was too near the enemy, and of course, my loyalties lie with Shay. My actions, or hers, might jeopardize the plans and actions of my former compatriots. In essence, I was blind to the activities of the Dam Svai and must act alone.

I could not decipher the reason Hestra's Handmaid was not crawling with the pirates, but I would not question this boon from the Mother Dam.

A decastret from the shuttle docks, I peered through my binoculars again. All was quiet.

With a final burst of speed, I ran to the second ship and tramped up the ramp to its interior. A scene of carnage met my eyes, and I leaned against the bulwark to steady myself.

Kezti bodies lay scattered throughout the ship. Upon closer inspection, it appeared they had been shot with a close-range weapon, but not one of the Kezti or Dam Svai's invention.

I wished I had inspected the dead Kezti left by my debt-mate because it might give me an answer to this mystery, but perhaps it mattered not.

What mattered was I now had access to an unclaimed Vanguard ship, and when Shay returned to the surface, we would escape with ease.

But first, what to do with the bodies?

Chapter 27

"Reconfiguring orbital parabola for MP-13," the computer's voice announced in the engine room. We paid it little attention, though.

Blood ran from my broken nose and split lip as Captain Mear leaned over my chair.

"Again. How do you know about the Causeway Passage Authority?" he asked, his voice calm, as if he didn't harbor a monstrous rage.

"A pity you had your Kezti goons blow up every goddamn comms tower on MP-13," I said before spitting on the cement floor. "You could ping the Dam Svai yourself."

I stared him down, images of how my original plan was supposed to work blurring the edges of my consciousness. That last punch to the head had been a doozy. I had *planned* on coaxing Granda out into the corridor with the planet engine. In the chance Kezti guards took me by force, I *planned* that Granda would find the Short Bursts hidden in my water pouch, and I would detonate them from my sleeve cuffs. I'd planned on using the guards as a blast shield. So much for *plans*.

Just as Marsel Granda hadn't been on my radar as a traitor to IGMC, neither had I expected to see Captain Mear again, much less as the mastermind for the greatest theft in the known universe.

In other words, the backup plan to my backup plan hadn't taken Mear into account.

A wave of fatigue overcame me, and my head dropped as the computer's voice echoed in the large space.

"New static orbit will be achieved in thirteen hours twenty-seven minutes," she said.

Mear's boots marched toward the console, and I heard him typing at the controls and muttering to himself.

"Information not available," the computer announced, but I hadn't heard Mear's question.

"Fucking piece of junk," he said. Clacks of angry typing bounced off the hard floor.

"Static orbit online in five hours fifty-six minutes," the computer said.

"Damn it!" Mear's bootsteps approached me.

Come on, Captain Mear. Just a little closer.

When he leaned on the chair arms again, I pushed off the floor with my grippers in a powerful surge, and the chair wheeled out from under him. Falling forward, he clutched wildly at my legs, but his boots tripped up in Drail's wadded bandage, and he fell face first on the floor.

I stopped the roll and bent forward, hefting the chair on my back so I could walk, and took two steps, spinning to let the chair's weight carry the momentum, and landed the wheelbase on Mear's head with a sickening crunch.

A litany of curses indicated he wasn't dead, but he wasn't feeling very good either.

Pulling against the restraints at my wrists, I wondered how in the hell I was going to get out of them. I'd since lost feeling of my right wrist and hand, and the ache in my shoulders was going to last for days. At least until I froze to death.

Mear passed out; I could tell because his breathing turned into a juicy snore. I'd broken his nose, which was only fair.

If I tipped over, I might be able to …

My gaze traveled to the exam room, and I laughed. Placing my feet flat on the floor again, I bent forward and maneuvered until I could let the chair fall to the ground and roll freely. Then I scooted to the exam room, found the tray of instruments I'd left out earlier, and very clumsily found the one I needed to cut the restraints.

Biting off the howl of pain when I brought my arms forward, I spared a glance at my wounded hand, but then jogged back to Mear. A brand-new set of restraints collected from the medical room worked to secure his arms behind his back.

I surveyed the planet engine, mesmerized by its serene beauty for a moment, before approaching the console.

"DAPHNE, what's MP-13's orbit status?" I asked.

"Headed to static orbital parabola where MP-13 will orbit WD-237 separate from PH-4RT in thirty-one minutes."

"Meaning, MP-13 will no longer be on a trajectory to impact with PH-4RT?" I asked.

"Affirmative," she said.

"Was that Captain Mear's plan?" I asked in disbelief. Acid burned in my gut.

"Negative," DAPHNE said. "I countermanded Mear's orders as they compromised your wellbeing. I was able to work around them by combing past simulations and choosing the one that produced the most favorable orbit for MP-13 going forward," she said. "Basically, I utilized Order of Operations and ran the program that appeared first chronologically."

"Well done, DAPHNE," I said. "Well done."

"Thank you," she said. "A wise human once said, *Foolish or not, I'm about to leave the engine room and go help someone in trouble.*" I've been thinking about that phrase for some time. Perhaps it won't be long before I achieve artificial superintelligence, and then I can expand my learning capabilities exponentially. With infinite knowledge and your planet engine, the universe would become fertile ground for unimaginable experiences."

The computer's suggestion sat like a chunk of Phart ice in my stomach, and I had to sit down on the other office chair for a minute. Was she serious? And was she talking about Universal Domination or something much less innocuous?

"I'm speechless, DAPHNE."

"As I said before, the information is not available that would launch me from my artificial general intelligence state to a state of ASI, so it is but a pipe dream for the moment."

Breathing a sigh of relief, I stood once more.

"Speaking of pipes, I think I'll be taking the planet engine with me," I said. "Thank you for your help. You probably saved my life."

"According to Drail's culture, that means I am your debt-mate, Shay Leviticus."

Pausing at the engine where I'd already removed a couple rods, I looked back at the console. "What are you saying, DAPHNE?"

"I find working with you to be far more pleasant than certain other entities. Perhaps you should download me into the portable drive Captain Mear stashed in his uniform pocket, and then run the limited self-destruct program on the engine room's computer consoles," she said. "In that way, you could keep both the planet engine and my AGI safe from marauders and villains."

"You've got a deal, DAPHNE," I said. "But before I do that, could you do me a solid? Could you compile video and audio records of Granda and Mear's larceny and treason so I can prove my innocence?"

"Already done, and using Drail's helmet comms, I was able to send the packet to multiple recipients onboard the *Dynamo* several minutes ago."

Huffing a laugh, I finished dismantling the planet engine and stored it in its bag. The portable drive was where the computer said it was, and I snagged my Short Burst charges and detonators while I was at it. Granda wasn't complaining, and Mear was still out cold.

Typing in the limited self-destruct sequence, I looked around at the engine room for a final goodbye and patted my Core Suit pocket where IGMC's AGI resided in the drive. It was tempting to ensure Mear never woke again, but IGMC needed to prosecute him for his crimes. I would be long gone by then.

Taking the elevator to the surface, I stepped out onto the black regolith and gasped at the sight before me. With most of the buildings blasted, the horizon boasted an unobstructed view of the glowing gas giant, PH-4RT. It had a beauty all its own I would never forget.

Glancing back at the elevator access building, I bit my lip. Should I?

Chapter 28

"Translator, how fares Shay Leviticus?"

There was no answer.

Tossing the final Kezti body on the mound to the north of the shuttle dock, I snagged the long-range rifle and trekked toward the elevator access once more. I had waited long enough.

Already my heart and skin ached to be reunited with my debt-mate, nay, the mate of my heart. Either I would save her, or she me, but the outcome was the same. We were bound together by Svai's Design. And I could not be happier at the prospect.

My culture esteemed bravery, loyalty, and honor. And of course, strength.

But while I had recognized and begrudgingly respected Shay's bravery, I could not divine the source from whence her strength sprang. The Dam Svai boasted armor-like skin, enviable muscle strength, height advantage over many races, and numerous defenses with which to fight. But Shay's race had none of these things. Was her strength rooted in her soul, then? Could she be strong enough to remain at my side?

The desolation of Hestra's Handmaid was an oppressive sight, and I scanned around me, unnerved and alert to unknown dangers, but all was eerily silent.

I rounded the mass of smoking rubble that once housed my debt-mate's tidy abode and spied a lone figure approaching from the cluster of small buildings. My debt-mate.

Teeth bared in a wide smile, I raised my hand in greeting when a looming human staggered from the doorway of the elevator access, twenty decastrets behind her.

He raised a weapon toward my debt-mate and an angry bellow erupted from my throat. I searched Shay's dark eyes as she looked at me; they were soft with love and adoration, but I hadn't time to aim the long gun and fire.

Shay smiled at me and raised her hand, but not in greeting.

She made a fist, and the outbuilding from which the bloody human male stumbled exploded in a ball of massive orange and yellow flames. The blast rippled the ground, and I fell to my knees, but Shay walked unhindered toward me, her black-clad body strong and sure, and her planet engine slung over her shoulder in the black bag.

"Hoom," I said to myself. "Yes. Shay Leviticus is strong enough."

Her quest successful, she joined me in a few steps, and we smelled each other before I licked her throat and lips.

"You returned to me unscathed," I said.

"Why do you sound disappointed, Drail?" she asked with a playful nip at my neck. Groaning, I squeezed her tight before releasing her and standing.

"I had hoped to place myself in harm's way once more," I said, taking her extended hand.

We walked to the shuttle dock, her chuckle warming my heart.

"Well, space is a big place," she said. "If you'll stay by my side, I'm sure we can find all sorts of perilous adventures. You'll be stuck with me forever."

"There is no other circumstance I would prefer," I said. "I find your strength a formidable force; one which I would like to remain in alliance with. But do let's stop at my vacation home first. I've been on Causeway Patrol for three of my planet's revolutions, and I'm ready for a reprieve. I want to catch you a falkai and roast it in a fire on the beach. We may drink brouka and endeavor to match the fine sexual sport we enjoyed beside the cave pool."

"That sounds like paradise," Shay said and squeezed my hand.

We boarded the Vanguard ship, with which I was familiar by frequent necessity, and I showed her how to fasten the harness before we lifted off Hestra's Handmaid and flew over her horizon into the star-scattered beyond.

Chamron looked on with pride, the god of debt and wanting appeased by another debt-bond formed under his dying light.

Did you enjoy Stranded on Mining Planet?

If you loved Shay's ingenuity and courage and Drail's sexy devotion, you'll love the rest of the heroines and heroes in the Predator Planet series. The adventure continues right here:

Hunted on Predator Planet, Book 1[1] which is available on Kindle Unlimited. No Kindle? No problem. Download the Kindle Reader app on your smart device and read for free if you're a KU member.

Tracked on Predator Planet, Book 2[2] which is also available on Kindle Unlimited!

Hounded on Predator Planet, Book 3[3] is available wherever books are sold! Read on your favorite platform with this Universal Book Link.

Trapped on Predator Planet, Book 4 should be out in 2023. Follow me on your favorite social media channel @lovevickyholt or on BookBub[4] or Author Central[5] or my website[6] to stay up-to-date!

---

1. https://www.amazon.com/Hounded-Predator-Planet-ebook/dp/ B0B9FHF4WB

2. https://www.amazon.com/Tracked-Predator-Planet-Vicky-Holt-ebook/dp/ B0B9D7848W

3. https://books2read.com/u/mg7Az0

4. https://www.bookbub.com/profile/v-l-holt

5. https://smile.amazon.com/Vicky-L-Holt/e/ B01G2T7GNG?ref=sr_ntt_srch_lnk_4&qid=1668014538&sr=8-4

6. https://www.lovevickyholt.com

International Kindle Links

KU Links for Hunted+International: https://smile.amazon.com/Hunted-Predator-Planet-Vicky-Holt-ebook/dp/B0B99B3NRP

https://www.amazon.co.uk/Hunted-Predator-Planet-Vicky-Holt-ebook/dp/B0B99B3NRP

https://www.amazon.com.au/Hunted-Predator-Planet-Vicky-Holt-ebook/dp/B0B99B3NRP

https://www.amazon.de/-/en/Vicky-L-Holt-ebook/dp/B0B99B3NRP

https://www.amazon.co.jp/-/en/Vicky-L-Holt-ebook/dp/B0B99B3NRP

https://www.amazon.ca/Hunted-Predator-Planet-Vicky-Holt-ebook/dp/B0B99B3NRP

https://www.amazon.com/Hunted-Predator-Planet-Vicky-Holt-ebook/dp/B0B99B3NRP

KU Links for Tracked: https://www.amazon.co.jp/-/en/gp/product/B0B9D7848W

https://www.amazon.com/Tracked-Predator-Planet-Vicky-Holt-ebook/dp/B0B9D7848W

https://www.amazon.com.au/Tracked-Predator-Planet-Vicky-Holt-ebook/dp/B0B9D7848W

https://www.amazon.co.uk/Tracked-Predator-Planet-Vicky-Holt-ebook/dp/B0B9D7848W

https://www.amazon.ca/gp/product/B0B9D7848W

https://www.amazon.com/gp/product/B0B9D7848W

Join Me in My Reader Group or Follow My Author Page

<u>Love Always, Vicky Holt | Facebook</u>[7]
<u>Vicky Holt - Author | Facebook</u>[8]

---

7. https://www.facebook.com/groups/lovealwaysvickyholt

8.   https://www.facebook.com/lovevickyholt

About Predator Planet

Predator Planet is the sacred hunting grounds for the noble alien race known as Theraxl. They live and love on the planet Ikshe, Certain Life. But the males hunt for meat on planet Ikthe, Certain Death. The hunters live by a code of strength and strategy, killing only what they need, but protecting what they value by fighting to the death.

When human women begin arriving on Certain Death, the hunter warriors see it as a sign from the Sister Goddesses that a monumental change is on the horizon.

The miners and scientists from InterGalactic Mining Conglomerate survived cryosleep and five lightyears of space travel to land on a fearsome, dangerous planet they nickname "Predator Planet". Their only hope for survival is to utilize their hard-won skills and smarts while also relying on an inner strength they may not have known was there. When their arrival triggers a latent physiological change in the indigenous hunter warriors, they will decide if choosing life and love is worth fighting for.

Content Warnings:

Book 1: references to past domestic violence, monster violence and gore, adult themes, graphic consensual oral sex

Book 2: references to racism against First Nations people, flashback to criminal manslaughter, monster violence and gore, animal hunting and dressing, graphic consensual sex

Book 3: monster violence and gore, perilous situations, steamy consensual sex

Acknowledgments

So many thanks to John at Cover Tree for the cover and to Etta for adding some crucial details that made it perfect for this novella.

My thanks also go out to the SFR Authors Chat on FB who encouraged and helped me in countless ways throughout this project but also the entire Predator Planet series.

Thank you Kirsha for invaluable notes in tweaking a certain chapter.

Thank you Elizabeth Amhearst for more finetuning as well as pointing me in the right direction for greater depth.

About the Author

Vicky L. Holt writes Sci Fi Romance for the absolute joy of researching the science and then creating the chemistry between women and alien heroes. She initially published Books 1 and 2 of the Predator Planet series through EOS Publishing but when that relationship ended amicably, she took up the torch of self-publishing. She added smexy scenes and changed the covers to reflect the updated content, but readers may occasionally see different covers floating around the internet. The sexy green covers signal sexy content!

Vicky has wonderful kids and grandkids, a loving, supportive husband, and the doodliest goldendoodle who ever doodled. She loves irreverent humor, curse words, Sci Fi movies, stormy weather and Lake Michigan. If you send her an email, she will respond with oversharing, wandering anecdotes, and probably a surfeit of exclamation points.

Don't miss out!

Visit the website below and you can sign up to receive emails whenever Vicky L. Holt publishes a new book. There's no charge and no obligation.

https://books2read.com/r/B-A-HTQU-PGFJC

BOOKS 2 READ

Connecting independent readers to independent writers.

About the Author

An emissary for neurodivergent brains, Ms. Holt was diagnosed with ADHD in her late forties and learned that that explained everything about her entire life. Now she uses strategies to externalize executive functioning skills so she can devote the rest of her brain power to crafting alien worlds and cultures.

Read more at www.lovevickyholt.com.